Clement
The Green Ship

Craig R. Hipkins

Published by Hipkins Twins

Clement: The Green Ship

Copyright © 2021 Craig R. Hipkins

www.hipkinstwins.com

Print ISBN: 979-8-501-53663-0

Library of Congress Control Number: 2021910205

Thanks and Dedication

I would like to dedicate this book to all my friends, old and new.

I would like to thank my editors, Tina Hipkins and Tracy Doby who always provide me with great feedback and encouragement.

Cover Art by: Adrián at www.adriandkc.com

Map 1

North Atlantic Ocean (Circa 1161)

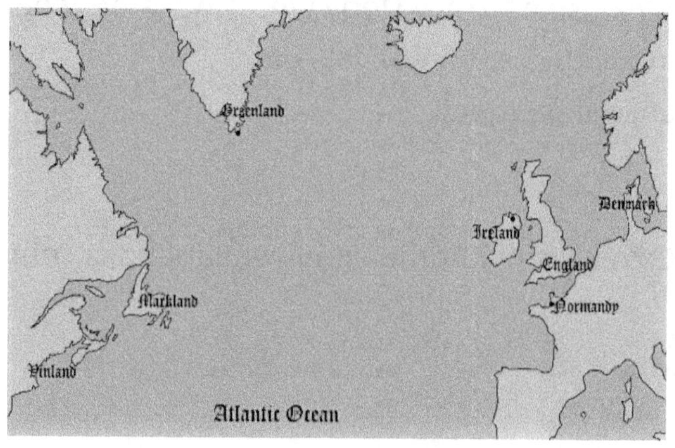

Map 2

Clement's Movement's in Greenland

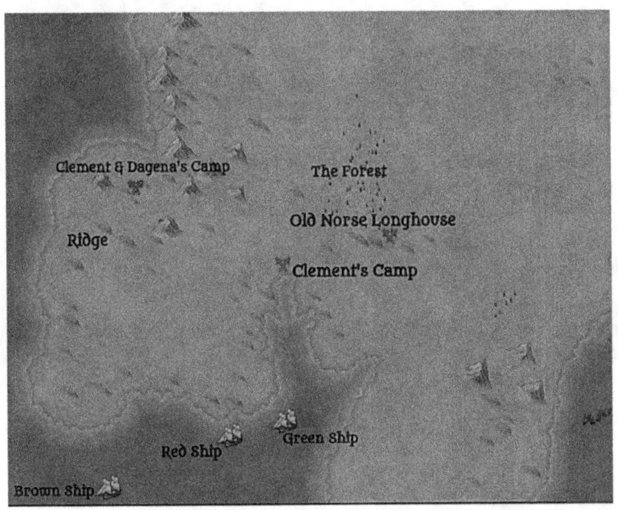

Chapter 1

Chinon castle sat on a high bluff overlooking the Vienne River in the Loire Valley of Touraine. It was a majestic and stately residence with whitewashed stone walls and towering turrets that stood higher than anything around them. From the top of one of the newly built towers, one could see a breathtaking view of the town and the bountiful vineyards and fruit orchards that dotted the countryside. It had been a few years since Henry Plantagenet had quarreled with his late brother Geoffrey and seized the castle, after having laid siege to it. Since that time, he had taken great efforts to fortify and add on to the palace. The additions included a massive hall and a small, decorated room where visitors were ushered in and told to wait until called into the king's presence.

In this room a teenage boy sat, looking pensive on a stone bench, next to a girl the same age. They had been talking, but the boy was no longer in the mood to hear idle chatter. Although the girl continued to speak, he was not really listening. He was thinking. A week earlier a messenger had arrived at the castle of la Haye with a letter stamped with the wax seal of King Henry. The letter was addressed to Clement, Count de la

Haye. He was to open the letter in the presence of no one and to keep its contents secret until he had counsel with the king personally. Upon reading the letter he was to burn it immediately and journey to the king's residence at Chinon with due haste.

He had sat in his dimly lit library, surrounded by scrolls, scientific instruments that he had been working on; and something else, a globe. There had been globes constructed since Roman times, but nothing like this one. This one was different. It implied that the earth was a giant orb and if a ship sailed east or west it would eventually return to its destination. This was dangerous ground to tread and the young fourteen-year-old count knew it. He was also aware that the sun and not the earth was at the center of the solar system. He had concluded correctly that the geocentric model of the ancient Greek philosopher Ptolemy was wrong. He had sat in his chair holding the letter and staring glumly at the globe, which was illuminated by the candles on the table and the glowing hearth providing him warmth from the chill outside the castle walls. He had crumpled up the letter and tossed it into the flames, which turned it to ashes within seconds.

Now here he was, a week later, sitting in the king's own antechamber, waiting for his majesty to see him. The girl sitting next to him had finally quit talking when she realized her audience was in a daze and not even listening. She playfully slapped him on the arm.

"Clement, wake up! You didn't hear a word I just said to you."

He glanced at her, an irritated look on his face.

"Dagena, forgive me. I have a lot on my mind right now, as if you do not know. It's not every day the king of England requests an audience with me."

She rolled her eyes and frowned. She was a tall girl with pale skin and a few freckles with long fiery red hair that she kept brushed back neatly on her forehead. She had delicate features. A small aquiline nose set over a mouth with thin lips and a narrow slender neck. She was wearing her best garments today, a green robe trimmed with silver.

"He's just a king," she said nonchalantly, studying the silver cross necklace Clement had given her on her birthday a few months earlier. She was twirling it between her fingers as if it were a toy.

"Just a king?" he responded incredulously.

"Just what I said. He doesn't intimidate me, Clement."

She pursed her lips and gave him another playful slap on his arm and smiled devilishly.

"Dagena, don't embarrass me in there. I beg you. Just let me do the talking," he said nervously.

"I won't embarrass you, Clement, but I am sure that King Henry will want to ask me questions. After all, I am going in there with you."

The boy cringed. "Only because you won't let me go in there alone."

She was grinning. "Well, you could order me not to go in. After all, you are a count. I am just a little kitchen servant," she said sarcastically.

Clement stood up and clasped his hands behind his back as he walked over to the open window. Peering out onto the veranda, he could see the crisp flowing Vienne. A paddle boat was visible with two occupants sitting close together. He wondered if the two were fisherman. Perhaps they were something else? Lovers perhaps? Dagena was watching him closely. When he turned back around. He was smiling. With an exaggerated walk he strutted back over to the bench and sat down next to her, leaning forward and resting his chin on his knuckles. He gave her a quick glance.

"What? Why are you smiling, Clement?"

He looked down at the wooden crate next to her and his eyes narrowed.

"Dagena, I am prepared to defy the king if I must."

Her face became serious. "How do you mean? I do not think that I understand you?"

"If...if he attempts to make me marry someone. Someone...well, someone besides you Dagena."

She was about to respond when the door of the antechamber opened and a servant of the king stood there. He was a drab looking man with a clean-shaven pock marked face. He glanced at the two youths, who had both stood up thinking that it might be the king himself who was calling on them.

"The king will see you now," he said cheerlessly. "My name is Bernard and I shall be your servant while you are here enjoying the hospitality of the king."

Bernard bowed and motioned for the youths to follow him. Clement picked up his crate, but the servant snapped his fingers and another servant appeared like magic.

"He will take care of that," Bernard said.

Clement handed it off and glanced at Dagena.

They looked at each other nervously, despite Dagena's bravado. The servant led them through the great hall and into a large banquet room. A large tapestry depicting a battle scene hung on the wall across from a magnificent looking hearth where a short lumbering man was busy adding fuel to the fire. Bernard and the other servant left, leaving the crate on a sturdy mahogany table. Clement and Dagena stood awkwardly, watching the man take an iron poker and push a log toward the back of the pit. This caused a shower of sparks to shoot up, a few of them scurrying across the stone floor.

"Bloody hell...pine! I've told them countless times to bring me oak and maple!" the man exclaimed sharply. His back was still to the fire and Clement wondered if he even realized that they were in the room. He was about to say something polite when Dagena beat him to it.

"Uh, excuse me, but we are supposed to be here to see the king not one of his servants," she said rudely.

Clement's mouth dropped and he suddenly thought about crawling under the table and hiding, but instead turned to Dagena with an exasperated look.

"Dagena! He is the king!"

The man turned and wiped the soot from his hands on his dirty wool tunic. He was rather short, but stocky and bow-legged with flaming red hair and a ruddy face. He was nearing thirty and was already slightly overweight. It was obvious that this was a man who had an appetite and enjoyed spending time outdoors and in the saddle. He glared at the two youths, still holding the iron poker. Slowly he advanced toward them, sizing them up and twirling the poker around as if he were going to bash their skulls with it. Their eyes wide. Clement swallowed hard.

"Sire, I apologize for the lady Dagena's remark. It was quite out of character," he said nervously.

The king stood in front of them with a stern countenance. He then pointed the poker at Dagena who naturally gravitated toward Clement for protection, grabbing hold of his arm.

"No. I don't think so," Henry said with a slight lisp. "I do believe it is quite natural of her to insult a king."

Dagena opened her mouth. "Your majesty, I am truly sorry for..."

He stopped her by holding up his free hand. Clement felt Dagena's hold on him tighten.

"Sorry for what?"

He looked at his soiled tunic, ripped hose, and worn-out boots and scratched his head.

"If I were a stranger coming to a castle and ushered into the presence of a king and came upon myself...well...I might just conclude that a peasant had broken in and was up to some mischief."

The two youths were rendered speechless but looked at one another cheerfully. Their nervous tension abating somewhat, the king put them at ease. Henry returned to the fire and placed the poker in its stand. He then rang a bell and almost instantaneously a man appeared from a hidden chamber behind them.

"Bring us some wine, figs and lampreys!" the king screamed. "And be quick!"

The servant bowed and quickly disappeared. Clement noted with dry amusement the servant's rich dress compared with that of the king. Dagena had a comical grin on her face, unnoticed by the king, whose attention was directed at the crate on the table. Clement pinched her arm and silently scowled at her.

"So! You are Clement, Count de la Haye?"

Clement's head turned sharply in the king's direction. "Yes, sire...but...but we have met before."

"Have we now? I do not recall. Perhaps you can shock my memory into remembering."

"At a tournament in Rouen a few years ago. I...I was with my father."

The king studied the boy. Clement had gotten taller. He was only a few inches shorter than the king, slim and wiry, but strong. He was wearing his best cloak, a green one, over a simple Saxon tunic and wool hose. His long wavy blond hair reached his shoulders. The king wagged a finger at him.

"How old are you?"

"I have just recently turned fourteen, sire."

Henry cleared his throat and folded his arms. His eyes looking upward as if he might be thinking. "I remember you now. You were but a small boy then. You have grown some. For the past year, I have heard about this boy count who led a peasant army against a rabble of brigands and highwaymen. However, I must tell you, I was told that he was near twenty years of age. One of his arms as big around as my chest!"

Clement swallowed nervously. "I...I am sorry to disappoint you, sire."

The king was once again looking at the crate, but sharply turned his head toward the boy.

"Disappoint me? Ah! How wrong you are! On the contrary, lad. If you have accomplished all the things that I have heard about over the course of the year and have done so in the slight body that stands here in front of me, I can only imagine what you might accomplish in the years ahead!"

Clement bowed politely. Dagena had crossed the room and was examining the tapestry.

"Do you like it, my dear?" the king asked, noticing her admiration of it.

"It is nicely woven, but the scene depicts death," she said. "I don't like death."

Henry chuckled. "Death is one of life's only certainties. It is noble to die in battle for your king. I am sure that the young count standing here would agree with me. But come! Let me get to the reason why I have called you here. Have a seat at the table. The refreshments are forthcoming."

As he said this, the door opened and two servants entered with silver platters and set them on the table. Henry sat down and plucked a lamprey from one of the bowls and used a knife to cut a section off it. He looked at it with a dubious stare before popping it in his mouth, then motioned with his hand for his guests to help him partake of the food.

"Fourteen, eh?" Henry said, licking his fingers after devouring another piece of the lamprey. "That is young…young indeed, but old enough."

Henry belched while grabbing a fig and wagged his finger at Clement.

"I need you to do something for me."

The boy looked at Dagena and leaned forward in his chair.

"I am listening, sire," Clement said quietly, his eyes narrowing.

"You possess a ship. I believe they call it the Green Ship."

The king hesitated and glanced at Dagena, who was eying him suspiciously.

"Indeed, sire, I read your letter. You require its services but were reticent on the details."

Henry took a swig of wine. "I understand that you also possess something else."

Clement leaned back in his chair and folded his hands in front of him. "And what is that sire?"

"An intellect superior to all others. My source tells me that you have amassed a library of sorts and spend hours perusing old scrolls and maps and can speak a dozen languages. That is why I asked you to come here and to bring your maps," he said, gesturing toward the crate with his greasy fingers.

Clement frowned. "But you didn't say why you wanted the service of my vessel, or the reason you want to borrow my maps."

The king smiled and leaned forward. His eyes cold and penetrating. "I do not want to borrow your maps. I want you to keep them. You will need them to help you find your way to where you will be going."

"I...I don't understand, sire," the boy said. "I was under the impression that you wanted to borrow my vessel to undertake a journey to a land far away."

Henry held up his hands. "And you are correct, but what I failed to tell you in my letter is that I want you to lead this expedition. You are to be my admiral."

Clement felt his heart beating rapidly in his chest. "Sire...it would help if I knew where I was going."

The king burst out laughing. "Have no fear about that, young Clement de la Haye! But tell me...did you bring what I requested?"

"I did, sire," Clement said, standing up and loosening the brass hatches on the small crate. He pulled out his globe and set it in front of the king. The globe was expertly built, swiveling on a triad of three silver balls. Clement had designed and built it over the course of a month. He had spent many sleepless nights pondering over and plotting the land masses he knew existed based on maps he had acquired and knowledge he had received firsthand.

"I am intrigued," the king said, marveling over the creative design. His eyes were wide and focused. He looked at Clement. "Can I touch it?" he asked.

"Of course, sire," Clement responded.

"You might want to wipe your fingers first, sire," Dagena added. She was glancing at the king's hands, which were covered in lamprey oil. Once again, Clement cringed.

"Oh, yes...pardon me," Henry said politely, dipping his fingers in a bowl of water and then drying them with a napkin. He gently turned the globe, inspecting the land masses and the seas. Each one was labeled in Latin. He then turned it to where there was nothing but blue ocean and artistic depictions of sea monsters and foundering ships. Among them he noticed a small sliver of land far away from any other land mass. He pointed to it.

"Vinland! Then you do know of it!" Henry exclaimed excitedly. "My cartographers were not wrong!"

Clement leaned on the table, focusing his gaze on the king, his face serious. "Sire," he said. "What is this all about? You must be frank with me."

The king walked away from the table to ring the bell twice. Instantaneously, another compartment opened and a tall man emerged into the room. He was raw boned, with square shoulders and a small head that seemed to be disproportionate with his large body. He was holding a long scroll and spread it out on the table in front of them.

"Lad, I introduce you to Trousett. He is one of my loyal servants who performs certain services for me. He brings me intelligence from within and outside of the realm. He knows everything that goes on. In fact, he is the one who brought you to my attention."

Clement looked at Dagena and frowned. "But how? I have never met this man until just now, sire."

Henry smiled, showing his yellowed teeth. "No indeed. He has agents who work for him. You will never know who they are. But that is not important."

Henry turned to Trousett. "Show him the map."

"Yes, sire."

Trousett turned to Clement and bowed. "Sire, it is a pleasure to make your acquaintance."

Clement nodded. "And yours too, sir. This is the lady Dagena." Clement said suddenly.

"My lady," Trousett said, bowing again, and then, forgetting about her, he turned to the map.

"The map's origins are unknown. A trader found it at the fair in Troyes last year," Trousett said.

Clement leaned forward with his elbows on the table. Dagena was looking over his shoulder. The map was detailed and showed the small sliver of land labeled Vinland surrounded by large expanses of ocean. The young man looked up at Henry, who was grinning. The king then pointed at the map.

"A few months ago, I was informed of a sea voyage preparing to leave the Bretagne coast when the leaves turned. A fleet of vessels led by a man named Sir Humphrey Rochford. Not much is known about him, though I believe he is working with King Louis as Trousett's agents have seen him in his company. The fleet is well equipped for a long voyage and is set to leave within a fortnight."

"To Vinland, I can guess," Dagena said, interrupting the king.

"You are astute, young lady, and correct. I want to find out the purpose of this fleet's mission and why they are sailing to this distant land."

"For exploration no doubt," Clement said, his finger tracing a line from the coast of Normandy to Vinland.

"Perhaps," Henry said. "But I don't think so."

"What do you think, sire?" the boy said, his eyes still perusing the map.

"I do not know, and that is why I am sending you in search of them. I want you to be my eyes and ears."

Henry's eyes narrowed. He was glaring at the boy. Clement finally looked up from the map.

"Sire, there is something I must tell you."

"By all means, lad,"

Clement returned to the globe, pointing to Vinland.

"Please do not take offense by what I am about to tell you. But your plan to find these vessels is not as simple as you might suggest."

"And why not? You yourself have plotted Vinland on your globe. Have you not?"

"Indeed, I have, sire, but there is one thing that I have not told you. My globe is not complete."

The king glanced at Trousett and then back at Clement.

"Explain yourself," Henry demanded.

"Sire, when I received your letter, I was still in the process of working out the problem that faced me. You see, in the previous century the

Norse sagas tell of another land called Markland. It was a land of abundant forests where the wild people dwelled! Sire, this land, I believe is an unknown continent perhaps bigger than the whole of all the lands of the known world!"

He had the king's undivided attention. Henry's eyes were glowing as if he had arrived at some epiphany. Clement was biting on his lower lip.

"Sire, have you ever heard of a land called Bracille?"

"Never..." the king said, his interest piqued. "But I am certain that you are about to tell me."

"Admittedly, it is a supposition, but there is a reference to it in a scroll that my grandfather acquired from a Genoese traveler over fifty years ago. There is also an archipelago of many islands found by a voyager named Máel Dúin. On one of the islands there are said to be large crystals, while another is said to be inaccessible as it is surrounded by a golden wall to keep people out."

The king took another drab of wine and nearly choked when he heard the word, 'golden.'

Clement ran his finger in an imaginary circle on his globe.

"What I am trying to tell you, sire, is that finding this Sir Humphrey Rochford in this vast unknown ocean full of many wondrous and mystical lands is improbable."

The king looked sullen and appeared to be thinking. He twirled the globe slowly and stopped it, pointing to Vinland.

"But Vinland, if they are headed here like my intelligence report claims, you can find it?"

Clement shrugged. "There is a reference in the Norse scrolls that states that this land is south west of Greenland. But how far, it does not say. It is conceivable that if the Green Ship sails in that direction that we might chance upon it."

Clement looked up at the king, who was rubbing his thick red beard. He began to pace back and forth around the table and finally ended up over at the hearth where he added a log to the fire. Dagena nudged Clement and made a funny face. The boy rolled his eyes and went back to studying the map that Trousett had brought in.

"Trousett will be accompanying you on the voyage. Whatever you need, tell him and he will get it for you," the king said, turning around and coming back to the table. "The details of this voyage will be held strictly confidential. Is your ship fit to travel immediately?"

Clement looked up from the map.

"Yes, sire. My carpenter is adding a special feature, but it should be ready within the next few weeks. This has all happened quite suddenly…"

The king interrupted him. "Young Clement, two of my galleys and a knar will be added to your fleet. My men will man them, but you are fleet admiral. Twenty of my best and loyal men-at-arms and sailors will serve on the Green Ship."

This time it was Clement who interrupted the king.

"Sire, with all due respect, no one serves on the Green Ship but my men, under my standard. There is no negotiation there."

Henry felt as if a crossbow bolt had struck him. His eyes became wide and his brow deeply creased. Dagena nudged the boy on the shoulder.

"Uh…Clement. He is the king, right? That is what you just told me," she said, wagging her finger at Henry.

Henry folded his arms and slowly walked around to Clement's side of the table. The boy had stood up to his full height with a look of defiance on his face. Henry stared down at him and for a few seconds looked as if he might throttle the boy.

However, the crease in his forehead lessened and, instead of thrashing him, he began to chuckle.

"You would defy your king?" he said imperiously.

Clement swallowed nervously and nodded.

"Yes, sire, it is a matter of honor...in memory of my late father. I shall still serve you faithfully, but with my men and no other."

Henry placed a hand on Clement's shoulder. "Then who am I to tell you otherwise? Let it be so, but Trousett will sail with you on the flagship. Or do you have a problem with this also?"

Clement glanced at the cartographer, who was watching the negotiating terms with keen interest.

"Sire, it would be my honor to entertain Monsieur Trousett on the journey. His skills may prove useful to me."

"Then it is settled!" Henry clapped his thick hands and plucked another lamprey from the bowl.

"Eat up, lad! Put some meat on those bones! You are going to need it! By the way, your vessels are being stocked with provisions as we speak. You will need to supply the Green Ship as you see fit, but your credit will have the king's seal."

Clement looked puzzled and Henry noticed this.

"What is it? Speak freely! You are now Admiral to the king!"

"Well, sire, I am a little confused, that's all. What is it exactly that you hope to find?"

"Just what I have told you. However, I have a message that you will deliver personally to the High King of Ireland, Mac Lochlainn. This will be your first stop on the journey. The letter will be sealed and opened only by him in your presence. I will also enclose further instructions in a second sealed letter only to be opened when you are one hundred leagues out at sea, after leaving Ireland. It is imperative that you follow these instructions."

The king insisted on entertaining his two guests and when they took their leave of him, he was full of wine and good spirit. They left the same way they had entered. Trousett escorted them out into the courtyard, where Clement had left his bodyguard of twelve men, led by the giant, Jacques, who stood nearly seven feet tall and weighed almost 400 pounds. He was a tower of strength and sheer muscle and the boy count relied on his protection. Clement handed Jacques a folded piece of parchment.

"Jacques, send this with our fastest horse to la Haye castle."

The giant scanned his men. He chose two from the ranks and handed it to one.

The courier rode off at a fast clip, followed by his companion. The letter, addressed to Wedem, Clement's garrison Commander, was written in Latin. It was a terse message.

"Have Olaf choose a body of knights and archers ready to ride to Harfleur upon my arrival. The details will be forthcoming."

Your faithful friend, Clement

Chapter 2

The smell of frying pork spread through the banquet hall at la Haye castle. Clement rubbed his tired eyes and yawned, swinging his feet over the side of the bed. It was a chilly morning. For a few minutes, he merely sat there looking out at the sliver of sunshine peeking through the shutter in his chamber. It had been a long night. He had perused the maps and scrolls and found a few that he had not previously read. He had added some land masses to his globe and plotted them on the map that Trousett had given him. Today was the day. He would leave and not return for a year, or possibly more. In fact, he might never return. So much could go wrong. He thought of the responsibilities that had been invested in him. He was the king's admiral at fourteen years of age. He was to lead a fleet of four ships, including his own, on a voyage to a land so far away only a few knew of its existence. Did it even exist? Were the references to the place called Vinland only stories told by some old sea dogs and taken for fact? He dismissed the thought. There were too many of them to discount from many different sources. He was deep in thought when he heard a slight tap on his door.

"Enter!"

A small wisp of a man with grey locks entered, carrying a tray with a mug of hot chicory water. Eustace, Clement's body servant, set the tray down on the table next to his bed and opened the shutter to bring in the bright rays of the morning sunshine. The boy squinted and turned his face away from the light.

"Your slippers, sire," Eustace said, retrieving a pair of felt ones from his closet and placing them next to Clement's feet. The boy slipped into them and stood up, grabbing his mug of chicory water and slowly moving over toward the window.

"Thank you, Eustace. I will miss this place."

"And I will miss you, sire," the old man said sincerely.

Clement stared out at the field where he had withstood two sieges within the last two years. One from a rascal who was called Marcoul the Bastard. He let his gaze roam to the lone oak tree near where the Templar knight, Adalbert de Langton had slain Marcoul in single combat. Then, last year, his own uncle, Sven the Terrible, had attempted to dispossess him of the castle. Sven failed, but somehow managed to slip away after a pitched battle in a snowstorm a few miles away. A lot had happened in the past two years, including the treacherous murder of his father before the first siege while he had been away on the Green Ship helping Adalbert and Halfdan locate a long-forgotten treasure in the great northern sea.

"Sire, your robe," Eustace said, breaking the boy out of his silent musings. He placed it over the young count's shoulders.

"Eustace, is Dagena still sleeping?"

The servant had a faint trace of a smile on his face. "Sire, does a hawk like to hunt from the sky?"

Clement's face lit up and he broke out laughing. "That was a foolish question, Eustace. I shall miss your witty responses to my ridiculous questions."

Eustace shrugged. "And I shall miss the ridiculous questions, sire."

"Alas, I can smell the pork frying. Let us retire to the hall," Clement said, still smiling.

A few minutes later, Clement found himself alone, seated in the hall relishing a plate of bacon and eggs. He was almost done with his breakfast when Wedem strolled over to the table to take a seat opposite him. The big Ethiopian prince had a worried look, which Clement was quick to note.

"Have no fear for my safety, Wedem. I shall be well equipped to handle any adversity on the Green Ship. As you well know, it is the best built vessel in the whole world."

He took a sip of his chicory water and raised his mug in salute.

"I am sending Captain Pierre with you," Wedem said. "I will feel better knowing that there is a solid knight there to give you counsel."

Clement cleared his throat. "I will have Olaf and Jacques by my side...and of course, Dagena. You should keep Captain Pierre with you, sir."

"I will not argue with you, Clement. Pierre goes with you. That is final."

The boy grimaced and looked down at his plate of food.

"Tell me, Wedem...do you trust me...I mean, what I am trying to say is... do you trust my judgement?"

"I trust it implicitly, but you are still young. I owe it to your father to care for your wellbeing. I cannot stop you undertaking this dangerous journey, as the king demands it, but I can still ensure that nothing ill happens to your estate in your absence.

Clement shrugged. "I understand, but...but say you were the king...would you trust me to lead a fleet of ships to a land many leagues distant?"

Wedem hesitated before speaking. "Clement, I have known you since the day you were born. To me, you will always be that young boy that I trained in martial skills and learned to love as if you were my own son. You are barely fourteen years of age. However, you have proven yourself over and over again. Trust yourself, and don't waver for a second, but take your advisor's counsel seriously."

The boy nodded. "I will heed your advice, Wedem. You have been like a father to me since my own father's death nearly two years now in the past."

As they were talking, neither of them noticed Dagena slip up on them from around the corner until she was right behind Clement. She covered his eyes with her hands.

"Guess who?" she said, with a sorry attempt at disguising her voice.

The boy smiled. "Well, let me see...it can't be Dagena because it takes a horn blowing in her ear to wake her from her slumber, so I must confess that I am mystified!"

She playfully boxed his ear. Wedem smiled and clasped his big hands behind his head.

"Olaf has everything ready," Clement said. "The archers and men-at-arms have been chosen. Marcel shall stay here and assist you, Wedem. He wanted to go, but if something should happen to you…God forbid…I trust Marcel's judgement. I suppose that you have already informed Pierre."

Wedem was grinning. "I told him the moment I received your letter from Chinon castle."

"I guessed that you would."

The boy turned his head around and looked up at Dagena, who had draped her arms around his neck.

"Are you ready?" he said, admiring her cheery face. Her cheeks were rosy with the morning chill.

"My trunk was packed last evening and the servants have already loaded it onto the wagon."

"Then I shall dress and we shall leave within the hour. It is imperative that we arrive at Tancarville castle by nightfall. Osment and Alice will be waiting for us."

The courtyard was alive and bustling with activity when Clement appeared from the archway.

He was dressed in a light cotton shirt with wool hose and a green hauberk over his shirt. It was emblazoned with the yellow lion passant, his family's coat of arms. On his head, he wore a green wool cap that Dagena had made him for his birthday. His long blond locks hung askew around it. He kept his bow with his quiver and arrows strapped to his saddle on the chestnut roan that Osment had given him the year before. He planned on riding the beast to Tancarville castle and leaving it to be cared for in the stable there. He would then proceed to Harfleur with Dagena, Olaf, Osment and Alice in the coach.

Dagena was waiting for him outside of the coach. She was dressed in a green tunic lined in silver and wore a green felt hat. She had brushed back her long flowing red locks and Clement smiled as he approached her.

"You look lovely today, Dagena," he said.

She held up her fist. "What, I don't look lovely every day!" she mocked.

He laughed. "Where is Olaf?"

"He is bringing your horse from the stable. Why don't you leave him here and you can ride with me in the carriage?"

"That will not do," he said cheerlessly. "The town folk expect to see me at the head of the column and I shall not disappoint them. Though why they should want to see me is a mystery. I am not much to look at. Wedem said I should try to fatten up on this journey."

She shook her head. "Well, I would disagree with you, Clement. I like you just the way you are."

Olaf arrived on his horse, leading Clement's roan by the bridle. He was a tall boy, a year older than Clement, and often mistaken for his older brother. A Dane by birth, he kept his blond hair cut short in the Norman fashion and liked nothing better than to ride his horse dressed in his martial attire. He was Clement's loyal friend and had proved to be so on several occasions since he had been rescued from a slave galley two years earlier in the English Channel.

"Where is your helmet, sire?" Olaf asked, handing Clement the bridle.

"It's in the carriage, Olaf. The thing gives me a headache, as you well know."

The Danish boy leaned across his saddle. "And if we are attacked along the way? Your uncle is still unaccounted for...as you well know," Olaf said, repeating Clement's words.

Clement threw his head back and grimaced. The thought of wearing the steel helmet all the way to Tancarville castle made him almost want to wretch. But he knew his friend was correct. Sven the Terrible might still be lurking in the vicinity. There had been sporadic sightings of him since he had disappeared a year earlier, but all investigations to bring him to justice had led nowhere. Although the chance of him gathering a force to ambush Clement's small escort were minimal, it still could not be discounted completely.

"Alas... Olaf is the bearer of wisdom once again," Clement said, ambling over to the carriage to retrieve his helmet. He pulled it onto his head and hustled back to his horse, nearly jumping into the saddle.

He turned to Olaf. "There, are you satisfied?"

"Completely."

"Sire, we are ready," came a voice from behind them.

Jacques had ridden up to the two boys on his massive warhorse, towering over them in the saddle. Beside him was Clement's standard bearer, and Pierre, his loyal garrison captain.

"Esteban and the archers will follow the supply wagons," Pierre said. "I will take half a dozen men and escort Dagena and the carriage while the rest of you ride in the vanguard."

Clement nodded. "Thank you, Pierre."

He scanned the men and women of the garrison who had assembled to see him off. There were nearly a hundred, but most would be staying with Wedem to man the castle and take care of the estate. Only twenty were going with Clement, a mixture of archers and men-at-arms. The men-at-arms all carried green and yellow shields and wore green surcoats with thick leather belts. They would accompany the young count all the way to Harfleur. Half would return with the horses while a few chosen would sail on the Green Ship.

There was a slight breeze blowing across the fields as the party left the courtyard. Clement looked back one last time and could see Wedem standing in front of the barbican looking downcast and depressed. He raised his arm in salute and Clement waved back. He felt a lump in his throat and felt sad, but he was quick to repress it. It would not do to have the men see him cry. He was too old for that. Dagena had the curtain open in the carriage, which made him smile. He knew she would have fun waving to the town folk, throwing them alms as they passed.

Clement's standard bearer was a tall man on a large black stallion. He carried the green flag with the yellow lion and cleared the way ahead of them with two picked knights in burnished chain mail. Behind them, rode Clement, flanked by Jacques and Olaf. Clement was distinguished not only by his hauberk but by the dyed green pheasant plumage attached to his helmet. His father sometimes had worn these decorative feathers and he decided he could honor him by doing the same.

The party left the castle behind them and rode down a small cart path that led to the first hamlet they would encounter. A pack of young children were the first to greet them, running alongside the horses, ringing small bells and stooping to collect coins that Dagena was tossing onto the dusty lane.

"Be careful of the horses," she yelled at them. Some of them were as young as three or four, which made the girl nervous for their safety.

The children, however, were attentive to the horses and found their parents and other town folk who had assembled in a pasture near a church. A priest, along with his servant, had come out to watch the procession pass. Clement waved at the assembled crowd and they cheered the boy count, who had only recently eliminated the threat of the highwaymen who had been terrorizing the countryside with impunity since the death of his father.

The party proceeded slowly at a canter and, as the day moved along, the sky turned an ominous grey. By dusk, as they neared Tancarville castle, a misty rain began to fall. Clement rode back to the carriage and called for Dagena, who peeked out from behind the curtain. She was yawning and had obviously been sleeping.

"Wake up, sleepy head," the boy teased.

She could see him leaning across the roan's mane and she smiled. She knew the cold rain was bothering him, but he would never ride in the carriage while his men braved the elements.

"We are almost at the bluff. Osment said he would send Milton the minstrel to meet us there to let us know if Lord Tancarville is out or not. If he is away then we shall go to the castle. If not, then he will secret Alice out in the dead of night and meet us here."

Dagena looked perplexed.

"But why didn't you tell me this before? You said we were to meet them at the castle."

Clement smiled. His horse wanted to push off again toward the front. He had to pull back on the reins to slow him.

"I didn't tell you because I didn't want to upset you that you might have to spend the night out under the stars," he said. His mouth curling, he winked at her.

"Clement, I don't care about that," she retorted. "As long as I'm with you. It will be exciting, don't you think? We will have Olaf, Alice and Osment, not to mention Milton, entertaining us. But just by looking out of this carriage we will be spending the night under the clouds and not the stars."

She cupped her hand on her chin, resting her elbow on the sill of the window. She could feel the misty rain on her arm, but it was not an uncomfortable feeling. In fact, she barely felt it. She was too busy admiring the shadowy figure of Clement, whose features were obscured by the twilight. She did not know that he was silently doing the same thing. He was about to say something to her when a shrill cry pierced the drizzly evening. It came from the front and instinctively Clement spurred his horse in that direction without even giving Dagena another thought. He arrived to see one of his men pinned under his horse, which had taken a tumble. The animal was in obvious anguish. Clement leaped from his mount and was about to start forward when Jacques grabbed his arm.

"Sire, don't get too close!"

"And why not?"

Jacques pointed to the man whose legs were pinned. He was completely still with his eyes wide as saucers. Fear had gripped him. Less than a foot away was the source of that fear. A serpent coiled and hissed, ready to strike at the slightest provocation. A giant slab of granite behind it prevented the snake from retreating in any direction except toward the prostrate man.

"That's an asp. One bite and he is a dead man, sire," Jacques said gloomily.

"Let's not give the wicked serpent a chance," Clement said drawing an arrow from his sheath and arming his bow.

"But if you miss?"

"I'll not miss."

He aimed and let the arrow fly. It was a direct hit. The arrow struck the serpent's triangular head, essentially decapitating it. For a short time, the assembled crowd of onlookers stood around watching the writhing snake until it finally was still.

Clement had lowered his bow and watched as Jacques used his massive strength to lift the horse while Pierre and Olaf dragged the frightened but grateful man from underneath it.

"That was an impossible shot, Clement!" Olaf blurted out.

The boy shrugged as if it happened every day and noticed Dagena standing behind him in the rain.

"What happened?" she asked, giving her attention to the wounded horse.

"Clement killed that asp with a single arrow. Right through the head!" Olaf exclaimed, emphasizing the point by poking his own head with his finger.

"The horse is in pain," she said, going to it and rubbing her hands through its mane as if that might relieve some of its suffering.

"The leg is broken from the tumble. We will have to kill it," Clement said.

"I...I will relieve it from its suffering, sire," Jacques said. "Everyone stand back."

Jacques straddled the horse and reached around its neck. Using his massive arms, he pulled back and, with a quick jerk, broke the beast's neck.

He stood up and Dagena noticed a tear rolling down the gentle giant's cheek into his thick beard. She ran to him and gave the big man a hug. Her thin arms were not able to reach around his huge waist.

"Well, let us continue on," Clement said morosely. "It is getting darker by the minute."

The party moved along the cart path until they reached the bluff where they found Milton all alone standing in the rain. However, when he recognized Clement, he snapped his fingers and Osment and Alice emerged from behind a thicket on the hillside. The redhaired boy was holding an umbrella over his cousin's head. When Olaf saw Alice, he became excited and leaped from his horse. They rushed toward each other and embraced.

"Alice, it has been so long!" Olaf exclaimed with excitement. He used his fingers to brush the wet strands of her dark hair from over her eyes.

She was smiling as he held her, the rain coming down a little harder, but it did not bother her in the least.

"Well, I guess this means that we will not have the pleasure of a cheery warm hearth inside the castle this evening," Clement said with an exaggerated frown.

"Oh, who cares," Alice said. "We can spend a lovely evening at a small woodman's cottage not far from here. I have already arranged it with the woodman's widow who is expecting us. Your men can stay in the old stable."

Dagena clapped her wet hands. "That will be grand!"

Milton the Minstrel stepped forward and bowed. Before Clement could stop him, he attempted to do a cartwheel but as usual bungled the stunt and ended up flat on his back. Clement approached and held out his hand which the minstrel took. Leaning back, Clement pulled him to his feet and shook his head with a smile.

"And it is good to see you too, Milton."

"And the feeling is mutual, sire," he said doffing his cap and bowing again.

"But let us not tarry here any longer," Clement said. "Where is this woodman's cottage kept by the widow that you speak of Alice? 'Tis not far from here you say?"

"Aye," the dark-haired girl said. "I shall ride with Olaf and will lead the way."

"But you will get soaked to the bone if you don't ride in the carriage, my lady," Olaf said with concern.

She took him by the hand. "Oh, Olaf, that doesn't concern me. We will dry nicely by a warm fire in no time. Come now!" she said, leading him toward his horse. "Let us lead the way!"

The party was soon on the move and Alice, true to her word, led them to a small cottage on the edge of the forest. A dim light could be seen from within. When the door opened as they entered the yard, the comforting warm brightness showed the silhouette of a stooped elderly woman waiting for them. Behind her, looming in the shadows, stood the lumbering form of a gigantic man.

Chapter 3

Olaf was the first to dismount and he helped Alice from the saddle. Taking her by the hand, they entered the cabin followed by Osment and Pierre, who handed off their mounts to a few of the soldiers. Clement had ridden back to the carriage for Dagena and had told the men of his guard to make themselves comfortable inside the old stable. The rain had slackened somewhat and was now only a gentle mist. Clement and Dagena arrived to find Jacques sitting on a stout wooden bench in front of the cabin. He was picking his teeth with a piece of wood.

"Are you not coming in, Jacques?" Clement asked.

"No, sire. I will stand guard and get Esteban to relieve me when the dipper gets there," he said, pointing to the cloudy night sky.

The boy count was confused. "But you can't see the dipper tonight, Jacques."

The giant winked. "Maybe not. But I know where it is all the same. Oh, sire, if the widow can spare a mug full of hot chicory water, I would be grateful."

"I think that I can arrange that, Jacques. Maybe a bowl of porridge to go with it?"

Jacques winked again and the two youths went inside. It was a homely place, with an open hearth on the far wall. There was a small table and only two chairs, one of which was already occupied by Pierre, who was pulling off his boots.

The widow was a tall matronly looking woman nearing sixty. She had grey eyes set over a crooked nose and a wrinkled mouth and had a cough that seemed to come from deep within her chest. The gigantic man who they had seen standing behind her was not a man at all, but a big offish looking boy of seventeen, who stood nearly as tall as Jacques and almost as wide. He had a thick crop of brown hair, small eyes and a large forehead. Clement recognized him immediately as being impaired of mind.

"Sire, I am Agnes the widow and this boy here is my sole surviving son. His name is Adam."

Adam was nodding his head and stepped forward. He grabbed Clement's hand and began shaking it wildly. Clement tried to pull away, but the grip was strong and he felt like his hand was being crushed in a vice.

"I am a woodcutter...I'm a good woodcutter!" the lubberly boy said. His mouth twisting in a happy grin. "I'm friends with Clement. Momma says that Clement is a king! But Clement is a little boy too."

"That is quite enough, Adam. Let Clement's hand go," Agnes said, touching the big boy's wrist.

He immediately let it go and Clement looked at his twisted hand in disbelief. He rubbed it with his other hand.

"I am sorry about that, sire, sometimes the boy gets carried away. He doesn't know how strong he is."

Clement smiled, showing his teeth.

"That is quite all right, madam. I am happy to be Adam's friend. But can I get some chicory water for my other friend who sits on the bench outside, and perhaps a little gruel for the stomach? He is...well... a rather large man and requires a lion's share of food."

Agnes nodded. "Of course, sire." She then broke out into a coughing fit.

"Are you well, widow?" Dagena asked, compassionately placing a comforting hand on her back.

Alice had risen from her place by the fire. "Let us make the chicory water," Alice said. "Come have a seat by your fire and Dagena and I shall make something to soothe that throat of yours."

It was not long before the widow was enjoying a mug full of brew and Jacques busy wolfing down a bowl of porridge. With the rain spattering off the thatched roof and the fire blazing its warmth with crackling pops from the dry wood, it was a homey feel to the evening. Alice sat with her head resting on Olaf's shoulder while Dagena and Adam watched Clement and Osment play a game of knucklebones.

"Your father is at Tancarville castle?" Dagena asked Alice.

"Indeed, and he is not too pleased with me, if I should say so," she responded. "He expects me to be married to Lord Clement when we come of age, but I have told him about Olaf and how we love each other, but he silenced me. He told me things that hurt my feelings, but I am done with him."

Olaf's face turned serious. "What...what did he say to hurt you so?"

She turned to the Danish boy and looked into his eyes.

"I don't want to hurt your feelings, Olaf. So, I won't repeat it."

"You won't hurt my feelings, my lady. I probably know what he said. So, I guess you can remain silent as I would not want you to feel hurt by repeating what he probably said."

Dagena threw her hands in the air.

"Who cares what he said? We all know that Olaf is the son of a fisherman and I the daughter of servants. Does it really matter?"

Clement was shaking one of the knucklebones in his hands and let it go, missing by a few inches. Osment clapped.

"Of course, it doesn't matter," Clement said, eyeing the knucklebone in Osment's hand. "By this time next week, we shall all be sailing into the unknown, far removed from courtly etiquette and set on an adventure that makes life worth living. Tis a challenge for us all. Am I correct, Dagena?" he asked, picking up another bone.

She grabbed the knucklebone from the palm of his hand and threw it in the air.

"Life is a challenge," she remarked with a chuckle. "Just look at Captain Pierre over there slumped against the wall, snoring like a wild drunken sailor. It is a challenge for him to sleep while we sit around and play games."

"I want to play! I want to play!" Adam exclaimed, squeezing his bulky frame between Clement and Osment, who shifted to the side to make room for him. The big lad was wearing a broad smile with his thick bottom lip drooping. His small beady dark eyes darted back and forth from Clement to Osment, as they watched him with amusement. He set his sights on Osment.

"Who are you? I do not know you. Who are you? Why is your hair orange?"

Osment looked at Clement and the two boys' burst out laughing. Adam was confused at their reaction at first but it was soon contagious and he joined them in their mirth.

"His name is Osment," Clement said, finally getting control of himself.

"Is Osment my friend too?"

Clement nodded. "Yes, Adam, Osment is your friend too."

"Is Osment a king like Clement? Why is Osment's hair orange?"

"It is red, not orange," Osment said sharply.

He reached over to touch the red headed boy's hair, but Osment drew back. Clement placed a hand on his shoulder.

"No, Adam, you cannot do that. Osment does not want you touching his hair. Do you want to play a game of knucklebones?"

He turned to Clement and in an instant, he had forgotten all about Osment's red hair.

"Oh, yes! Oh, yes! I want to play! Show me how to play!"

"Of course, we will, Adam. Have you never played before?"

Adam grabbed one of the pieces and studied it curiously. His simple mind attempted to process what it was.

"It is a bone," Clement said. "There are many games that we can show you, but we will start with an easy one."

The lubberly boy became animated and, much to Clement's surprise, was an astute learner. They played for the better part of an hour before everyone decided to turn in for the night. The widow offered her small, feathered bed to the two girls but they refused to take it out of concern for her delicate state. Instead, they curled up in wool blankets next to the fire. It was a cool crisp night and Clement, wrapped up in his cloak, listened to the howling wind gusts outside, sometimes whistling through a crack in the ancient cabin's thin walls. He wondered if Lord Tancarville and Lord Mowbray, Alice's father, would send a search party. Alice had left her father a note, informing him of her intentions. Milton was to deliver it. Clement considered the repercussions of this. The girl had told her father she intended on visiting castle de la Haye with her cousin Osment acting as her chaperone and protector. Never mind the fact that Osment was only fourteen himself. Alice was careful not to mention she would be sailing off into the unknown. She conveniently left this part out. She also neglected to tell him about Olaf. He knew of their long-distance correspondence after intercepting one of the boy's letters. He forbade her from ever seeing him, as he considered Olaf, the son of a Danish fisherman, to be beneath her station and dignity. But Lord Mowbray was not a stupid man. He would understand the real reason his daughter was going to visit the castle de la Haye, and it was not a social visit with the young count. Clement soon realized he was the only one still awake. It was always like that. He could never turn his mind off and just let it shut down. Every time he started to doze off, the widow would cough, a deep gurgling sound that seemed to come from beyond the grave. It did not seem to affect anyone else as he could still hear their light snores, all except for Adam, whose noisy exhalations sometimes sounded like a trumpet.

He heard voices outside the door. That would be Jacques being relieved by Esteban. The door then opened, letting in a cold rush of air. He knew it was Jacques by his heavy tread. The big man curled up in his cloak next to the door and was soon fast asleep. Clement envied his ability to do such a thing. He finally had enough and sat up. For a few minutes, he just sat there with his back against the wall, listening. It had quit raining and only the wind still rattled the trees outside. It was no use. Maybe a walk would help. He laced up his boots and quietly exited the cottage. The first thing he noticed was the full moon. The sky had cleared. Esteban was sitting on the bench with sleepy eyes and when he saw Clement his eyes became big and he bolted upright.

"Sire. What are ye doing out here at this time of night?"

Clement shrugged. "I suffer from insomnia, Esteban. Go inside and get some rest. I will take the watch."

"Are ye certain, sire?"

The boy nodded while adjusting his green wool hat. "Aye, tis a balmy night but I think I will take a little walk."

"Are ye armed? Where is your bow? Do ye want to borrow mine?"

"I have my dagger, Esteban. I'll be fine."

"I'll leave me bow and quiver on the bench, sire. But if ye need me, ye need only to call."

Clement was soon alone and decided a stroll down the cart path would be beneficial to his restlessness. Sometimes, it felt good to be alone listening to the sounds of nature at night. He ventured down the path in the direction they had come earlier. Looking back, he could see a slight wisp of smoke coming from the chimney. The fire had been blazing when they had turned in, but when he left there was nothing but a few charred logs and hot coals. Someone must have added a log or two. He climbed to the top of a small hill, feeling the wind at his back. A large pine tree had fallen near the crest of the hill. He was about to swing his leg over it when a noise from behind him caught his attention. He reached for his dagger and turned.

"Dagena?"

She was lifting the bottom of her tunic as not to trip over a branch of the fallen pine and looked up at him with a smile.

"I heard you talking to Esteban," she said. "I cannot sleep either."

"Well, you sure fooled me. I thought I recognized your almost silent snores."

Her eyes narrowed and she held up her fist.

"Are you saying that I snore?"

"Oh yes, Dagena, as loud as a horn in battle," he teased, his mouth opened in a wide grin in expectation for her mock retaliation. But instead, she wrapped her arms around him. He kissed her on the cheek and held her. They sat down on the wet tree trunk with her head resting on his shoulder.

"Clement, do you really think that we are going to find this land? The place called Vinland?"

He was shaking his head.

"I don't know, Dagena, but the Green Ship has been refitted with some new marvels you will find fascinating. If anyone can find this place, I can in the Green Ship. Just wait until you see the new renovations." Then he looked down at her with a worried expression.

"Do you not trust me, Dagena"

She did not look up at him but kept her head buried in his shoulder.

"Oh, yes, Clement. You know that I trust your judgement, but it is a long way away. When we ventured off on the Green Ship with Adalbert and Halfdan to that volcanic island, we got lucky."

She lifted her head, her fiery red hair and bluish green eyes appearing magical and hypnotic, bathed in the moonlight.

"Is Gorm coming along?" she asked earnestly.

He pondered her question.

"No. He is too old to make a journey so far. But we shall visit him in Harfleur."

"I would like that, Clement. Maybe he can tell us some more of those mystical sea tales of his."

Clement became excited.

"Yes! Oh, how I loved to hear them! Although I wonder if some of them are just a bit exaggerated."

"Of course, they are," she said with a gleam in her eye. "But no matter! They are fascinating all the same."

They talked for a while until the moon disappeared below the tree line. They then returned to the cabin. Dagena went inside but Clement stood watch until he finally fell asleep on the bench. He awoke with a start and the first thing he noticed were the first rays of light seeping through the trees in the east. He must have been asleep for hours. But something had awakened him. He sat up and listened. And then he heard it again. A soft murmur from within the cabin.

"Momma? Momma?" the voice was feeble and weak, but unmistakably and distinctly recognized as that of Adam.

Clement rose and entered the cabin. Dagena and Alice were kneeling on the side of the widow's bed, while Adam was cradling his mother's head in his lap.

"Momma? Momma? Wake up, Momma."

Clement rushed over and Dagena turned around and looked up at him. Her eyes were red and watery.

"What? What is it? What has happened?" he asked, a strain in his voice. "Is she?"

Dagena nodded. "She...she must have died in her sleep."

"Momma...Please wake up, Momma,"

Adam carefully lifted one of the widow's arms and then let it fall lifelessly back on the bed. He had a confused expression, as if he did not completely understand the significance and reality of what had happened. Perhaps if he moved her arms, she might find the spark of life and rise from her eternal slumber. Instinctively, he knew that something was wrong but could not comprehend it. His mother had always been there. She had been the rock. He tried to move her arms again, but nothing. He looked around helplessly at Dagena and Alice and then noticed Clement standing at the foot of the bed.

"Momma won't wake up..." he said, desperately addressing Clement as if he could perform a miracle.

Clement felt a tear running down his cheek. By now Pierre, Olaf and Osment had turned out of their blankets, as had Jacques, who was rubbing his tired eyes.

"I...I am so sorry, Adam," Clement said sadly. His voice choked with emotion.

Adam slowly raised his head, looking up towards the ceiling. He raised his massive arms and closed his eyes. His lips began moving rapidly and a few tears began rolling down his cheeks. Clement did not know what to do. He merely stood there feeling helpless, still awash with a flood of memories from the day he found out his own father had been killed.

Adam opened his eyes and blinked a few times. He then lowered one of his arms but kept the other raised and pointed at a spot near the door.

"Momma has gone outside. She is smiling," he said.

"Oh! I can take no more. This is too sad," Alice said, standing up. Olaf immediately embraced her and she buried her sobbing face into his chest.

Clement cautiously approached Adam, who had risen from his place at his mother's bedside and stood looking awkward and lost.

"Adam?"

The giant boy turned to him. His mouth was partly open. He towered over Clement, who placed a comforting hand on his wrist.

"Your momma is with the angels now, but...but it is okay. There...there was a reason we came here. There is a reason for everything...I think," Clement said, trying to comfort his simple-minded friend.

Dagena had stood up and reached for Clement's hand. He took it and together they walked Adam outside into the sunny dawn. A rabbit burst forth from behind the woodpile. Its

white tail flashing as it bobbed along until it
disappeared into a thicket. Adam smiled.

Chapter 4

The Green Ship sat in front of the dock looking majestic with its new coat of dark green paint and yellow trimmed rails. It was the finest looking vessel in the harbor, and, indeed, one would be hard pressed to find its equal. There were two covered castles, one on the bow and a much larger one on the stern. It carried a single sail, but Clement's boatwright, Baldwin, had turned the cog into a galley as well. He installed a pair of massive oars that could be manned in a calm. They could be thrust out of two tightly sealed portholes and rested on high quality forged iron oarlocks. To steer the ship, Baldwin had constructed a rudder of the pintle-and-gudgeon style. It was solid and had proved seaworthy on many occasions.

The other vessels of Clement's fleet were much humbler. The king had promised him two galleys and a knar, which was a solidly built craft made of solid English oak from the king's forest. Baldwin had his carpenters build a small castle on its stern where the king's man, William de Bayeux would keep his headquarters. The ship's modifications had been constructed in haste, just as Clement had ordered. He had further instructed copies of his maps to be stored on the knar in case the flagship should encounter trouble. The two galley ships would hold fifty men each and be commanded by two of the king's officers, Roger de Montfort, and a loyal Greek mariner, Ceres. These, too, were equipped with small castles on the stern.

It would be a few weeks before the fleet would be able to depart. They would need to wait for a favorable wind and provisions needed stocking. In the meantime, the quay was bustling with activity as laborers and sailors set to work loading the vessels in preparation for a long journey. Each ship was to be equipped with at least a three-month supply of water and the Green Ship would carry a large crate of wine. Also, the vessels would bring barrels of salted pork and beef along with cheese, dried plums, raisins, beans, biscuits, and chicory for tea. They would supplement their fare by dropping nets in the sea.

It was a cool, crisp morning with the sun shining brightly over the harbor. Clement had set his headquarters up at his great aunt's residence. The elderly countess de la Haye lived in a large two-story clapboard house with her two servants and guard, which Clement dutifully paid for out of his own purse. The old woman was getting senile and was predisposed to being cantankerous. Clement awoke to the sound of her voice calling for one of her servants.

"Where is that boy? Tell him to get down here now!"

The sound of her shrill crackling voice had also awakened both Osment and Olaf, who were sharing a room with Clement. Only Adam remained unfazed, still snoring deeply, his long bulky form stretched out on a bearskin on the floor.

"You had better get down there, Clement," Osment said with a smirk.

The voice, once again, began booming from the downstairs parlor, where her aged and feeble form sat tapping her cane on the flagstones in front of the hearth.

"That boy sleeps too late! He is like his father, God rest his soul, always lounging about like a lazy dog!"

"That sounds serious, sire," Olaf said, winking at Osment. "If I were you, I would make haste before she gets really upset."

"I do believe she is going to give Clement a whipping. What say you, Olaf?" Osment remarked. Both boys burst out laughing. Clement was sitting on the edge of his bed rubbing his eyes, still half asleep. One leg had been thrust into his hosen in a half-hearted attempt to dress. His disheveled yellow hair covered his eyes. He held up his fist at them.

"I should have slept on the ship," he said quietly.

They heard footsteps and creaking boards on the stairs heading up to their loft and then a gentle tap on the door. It opened a crack and a bald head appeared.

"Sire, the countess requests your presence in the hall. She is quite adamant about it."

"Thank you, Willem, tell the countess I shall be down forthwith after I have dressed."

"Yes, sire."

Clement went to the basin to splash some water on his face and was soon ready to present himself to his great aunt, who could still be heard barking orders and complaining to the servants. Olaf followed him down the stairs while Osment stayed in the loft to help Adam. The countess was sitting in her chair facing the fire when Clement arrived. Dagena and Alice appeared from the adjoining staircase at nearly the same time. Both girls wore broad smiles. They had been awake for some time and had already become acquainted with the lady of the house.

"Aunt, here I am. I apologize for our late arrival last night, but it was a tedious journey and we were delayed somewhat yesterday by unfortunate events that were beyond our power," Clement said, bowing politely.

She craned her neck around, the grey eyes attempting to focus on the boy.

"Help me stand, child!" she demanded imperiously. "Let me look at you!"

He helped her to stand. She was hunchbacked and he could not help but notice how much she had aged in the six months since he had last seen her. Her wispy grey hair had thinned and there were large pockets of flesh under her sallow looking eyes. She was moving her lips as she examined him. She grabbed his arm and pulled his wrist toward her.

"You are too thin! You need to fatten up! And cut your hair, child!"

She turned to the bald servant who was dutifully standing near her.

"Get this child a plate of biscuits and bacon!"

Clement rolled his eyes.

"Aunt, I am fine; one biscuit and a slice of bacon will suffice."

"Nonsense!" she screamed. "Don't back talk me or I'll use this cane on your hide!" Her attention was then directed at Olaf, who was trying to hide behind Dagena and Alice, both of whom were doing their best to suppress laughter at Clement's expense.

"Who are you? And why are you so bashful? Come here this instant!"

She had forgotten about Clement and, with her back to her nephew, pointed toward Olaf, who was pointing at himself as if hoping she was directing her attention at someone else. Clement took the opportunity to make funny faces at Olaf, knowing it was his turn to feel his aunt's wrath. The Dane stepped forward and she sized him up.

"Whoever you are, you too need to be fattened up! What is the matter with boys these days? Someone help me sit down…"

She did not concern herself to ask Olaf his name. It was Clement who finally gave her the proper introduction. When her mood had quieted somewhat, she sat passively, nibbling on a cake while watching the flames of a fire burning in the hearth.

After breaking their fast, Clement and Olaf ambled down to the quay where they met Pierre supervising the loading of supplies onto the various ships. He was talking to Trousett and William de Bayeux, who had arrived in Harfleur a few days earlier with the king's men-at-arms who were encamped in a field nearby. William was a tough-looking bird with closely cropped red hair, with a bearded, chiseled chin that seemed to be made from granite. He was wearing a long black cloak with silver lining. He was obviously a man of some means and had found favor with the king. Clement immediately knew why the king had chosen him to come along; he was to keep a watchful eye on the young Count of la Haye. As the two boys approached, he grinned, sizing them up as if he were attempting to discern which one he was to take orders from.

"Sir William, may I present the Count of la Haye," Trousett said, bowing gracefully. "Count, I present William of Bayeux."

Clement held out his hand, which William grasped firmly with a leering look of superiority on his face.

"So, you are the boy count who has gained high favor with the king. I have heard a lot about you in the last year or more. I must confess, I imagined you to be a stout little brute." He smiled, showing his rotten teeth.

"Don't let his small stature deceive you, Sir William," Pierre said, coming to Clement's defense. "He will surprise you."

William's face soured as he glanced at Pierre with contempt.

"I should say that I look forward to having you serve under my command," Clement said forcefully. "I have heard wonderous things about your navigating skills. Let us hope we can work amiably together. But tell me, sir...how do you like the castle that my carpenter skillfully crafted for you on the Brown Ship?"

William was confused. "The Brown Ship?"

"Indeed, I have taken the liberty of naming the four ships under my command. You will take charge of the Brown Ship, while Montfort will take the Black Ship, and Ceres the Greek will handle the Red Ship."

William cleared his throat and adjusted his cloak, never taking his eyes off Clement.

"My cabin will suffice. But, why the extravagance, my young lord?"

"We will be traveling far, Sir William...very far. In fact, even I do not know the complete instructions of my king. I am to open a letter with the king's seal when we are a hundred leagues at sea beyond the Irish coast. I know where we are headed and so shall you and my two other Captains this evening when you join me for dinner at the White Gull. Until then, it shall remain my secret, aside from Trousett. He will be traveling with me on the Green Ship as my king requests."

Clement removed the green cap from his head and began fumbling with the cord. He glanced up at the mast of his proud ship and could see the standard of the house of la Haye flapping in the breeze. He wondered what William thought of him. He did not know, but he had an idea whatever his opinion, it was not favorable. William's demeanor told Clement all he needed to know.

William was sneering.

"I am not accustomed to taking orders from a boy who is young enough to be my grandson," William said suddenly. "But I am at the whim of the king and shall not falter in my duty to him."

Clement grimaced and shook his head.

"Concern yourself with the task you are assigned. With regards to respect, I shall have it from everyone under my command. If you heed my instructions, we shall get along. The king has appointed me to this post and like you, I shall not falter."

Sir William was about to respond when a loud booming voice rang out among all the hammer blows from the last-minute carpentry work aboard the Green Ship.

"How many times have I told yuh not to use green wood! Ye bloody fool!"

"Tis Baldwin's voice that I hear!" Olaf exclaimed excitedly.

A large round head appeared over the rail. Baldwin, the ship's carpenter was grinning as he espied Clement and Olaf.

"What are ye doing down there, my young lords? Do I have tuh send Bran down there tuh chase ye up here! The Green Ship awaits ye! Where is the Lady Dagena? Tis sleeping the day away?"

"It is good to see you too, Baldwin!" Clement hollered, followed by a chuckle. As he said this, a large mastiff came bounding down the plank and jumped on Clement nearly knocking him over before showering him with licks of his slobbering tongue.

"And you too, Bran!" Clement said excitedly, hugging the massive dog. Olaf joined in on the fun and the beast was soon playfully chasing after the older boy down the quay. A few minutes later, they were on board the ship. A couple of Baldwin's workmen were adding the finishing touches to a sturdy covering which protected the rudder man from the elements.

"This will give the poor wretch respite from a storm if we happen to encounter any on the journey," Baldwin said.

The carpenter barely stood four feet tall, but what he lacked in height he surely made up with intelligence and skill. He was also amazingly strong for his size and very few men were willing to test his wrestling skills. He had been underestimated by many men who failed to see this and they soon regretted their challenge.

Clement ran his hand along the smooth surface of the board.

"Tell me, Baldwin, did you manage to procure a spare sail and mast?"

"Aye, me lord. The mast is stored in two pieces below. It fits together by a strong brace. As for the sail, I found two that will suit the purpose. One of them is sorely used but can be mended back to serviceable condition with a thread and needle. Perhaps the Lady Dagena will find the work rewarding along the way."

"I heard that, Baldwin!" came a voice from behind them.

Dagena had snuck up on them, with Alice in tow. Baldwin bowed respectfully while chuckling lightly.

"I have a better idea," she said, placing her hand on Clement's shoulder. "How about if I show Clement and Olaf how to mend cloth and they can begin work this afternoon?"

"That's a good idea, Dagena!" Alice added.

Clement snapped his fingers and pointed at Dagena.

"You are a real piece of work, Dagena," he said, wearing a broad smile.

They entered the sterncastle. A small oak table, fastened to the deck with two benches, took up nearly a quarter of the room. There were six sleeping compartments: four on the starboard side, and two on the port. Each berth was enclosed and contained a bunk and room for a chest to be stored underneath. Clement, Olaf, Osment and Trousett would occupy the berths on the starboard side, while the two girls would claim the ones on the port side. There was also a small, enclosed fire pit built on flat stones with a flue. It provided the cabin with heat and served as a place to boil water and cook food. Baldwin had created a device to pump water from a tank, lest a fire break out, which was always a danger on ships at sea. Clement instructed Baldwin to mount his globe on the table and his maps and books stored on a small shelf wrapped in oil cloths to protect them. A crate with various nautical instruments was mounted to the deck and Clement had taken great precautions to secure these invaluable devices, some of which he built himself, including a lodestone compass and an astrolabe. Dagena and Olaf had watched him build the astrolabe, made from brass plates and decorated in elaborate detail. The workings of the device seemed almost magical to them, but they had trust in the young count's superior intellectual capacity. They wondered how he managed it but manage it he did.

After Baldwin showed them the improvements in the sterncastle, he took them to the smaller castle on the bow. There were two sleeping berths in this castle and it was also the place where Baldwin kept his tools, spare ropes, tackle, and a large chest containing wool blankets and various cloths. It would double as sleeping quarters for Baldwin and Pierre. Baldwin and Pierre would sleep in this castle. Jacques had insisted on sleeping below with the men. A sturdy stairwell led down to the hold, but Baldwin had created a stout tween deck where perishables and drinking water were stored in large casks. There were enough victuals to last comfortably for six months for the twenty-five people on board the ship. Clement had placed Osment in charge of the commissary and the red-haired boy had taken to the task with relish. He was creating a logbook of everything on board the ship and how it would be rationed out daily. There were still kegs and crates sitting on the quay, waiting to be loaded onto the ship. Osment had assigned a guard to watch over the supplies. Clement was still waiting for the crates of wine and the trinkets the king had promised that could be used for bartering. Plucking the oil lamp from Baldwin's stubby fingers, Dagena was the first one to climb down the narrow stairwell into the hold.

"I had forgotten how dark it is down here," she said shivering.

"I am not climbing down those stairs," Alice said, folding her arms and peering over the railing into the dark hole. Dagena held the lamp up.

"Isn't anyone else coming down? Oh, yes...I had forgotten...Clement is afraid of ghosts!"

Clement was wearing a devilish smirk and decided to have some fun.

"I think I'll just seal the hatch to the stairwell. What say you, Olaf?"

Olaf clapped his hands together and mockingly looked up at the cloudless morning sky.

"Aye, sire. I think it might rain!"

Trousett could see the look of disgust in his eyes when he glanced at Sir William. The two men had followed the youngsters up onto the deck, leaving Pierre to supervise the sorting of supplies. Trousett had already toured the vessel, but William had thought it prudent to wait until Clement arrived so as not to arouse any suspicion that he might be attempting to undermine the boy admiral's authority. William had attempted to persuade the king to put him in charge of the fleet, but King Henry was adamant. He needed the Green Ship and, like it or not, Clement de la Haye had somehow, at such a young age, managed to gain power and influence in the Norman region around Rouen. His influence also extended into the coastal ports, where they had heard about his swift suppression of Sven the Terrible's revolt and the arrest of the murderous highwayman known as le Diable.

However, regardless of Clement's accomplishments and superior intellect, the king also recognized he was still only fourteen years of age and tasked William with keeping an eye on the young fleet admiral. If he should falter, or prove inadequate to the task, he was to immediately take command. There was only one problem; despite William's excellent ability to navigate, he had never ventured beyond the coast of Brittania to the north, and the Kingdom of Leon to the south. Also, despite his age and experience, his skills at reading the astrolabe and knowledge of maps were rudimentary at best. In comparison, Clement, at the tender age of twelve, had been one of the leaders of the now infamous voyage of Adalbert de Langton and Halfdan the Dane to the legendary Island of Fire. He was also recognized as being an expert with the use of the astrolabe and was even a cartographer who knew something about the strange lands that lay well out into the ocean to the west. There were also rumors that Clement had invented various instruments that could do magical things. William had longingly looked at Clement's sea chest in the sterncastle with a jealous eye, wondering about the contents or what it contained.

Dagena bolted back up the steps, almost tripping over her long green tunic. Clement took off running across the deck as she playfully chased him around the perimeter until he finally gave up, letting her catch him. She whisked his cap off and threw it to Alice. The two girls played catch with it as Clement shook his head and wagged his finger at Sir William. The boy was beaming with childish delight.

"See, Sir William, what I will have to endure on this voyage!"

Sir William was stroking his salt and peppered beard.

"The sea is no place for women, sire...or children," he added disparagingly.

Sir William turned and left. Clement was biting his lip while watching him depart. Suddenly a devilish look crossed the boy's face.

"See you at the White Gull this evening Sir William! Clams and turnips!"

Dagena came up behind him, put the cap back on his head, and grabbing it on both sides, pulled it over his ears in a ridiculous manner.

"I'll give you some turnips! Rotten ones!" Dagena joked.

Clement spent the rest of the day perusing his maps in the cabin with Olaf. He decided he would take the one he had been working on to the White Gull, rolled it back up, and placed it in the oil cloth. When he returned to his aunt's house, he found her asleep in her chair and quietly tiptoed by her. He was to meet his three captains and Trousett, alone at the inn. The following hour, the rest of his party would join them for a feast. After he cleaned up and was about to leave, he felt a finger tapping him on the shoulder. He turned to find Adam looming over him with a big broad smile.

"Adam goes with Clement. Clement is Adam's friend."

Clement rolled his eyes.

"Sorry, Adam, but you need to stay with Osment. I have some business to attend to."

"Please! Please! Please! Adam wants to go with Clement. I will show Clement seagulls!"

Clement shrugged. "Ok, Adam, but when you get to the inn you have to be quiet because Clement has to talk to some important men. Can you do that?"

Adam was scratching his neck and became animated. He lifted Clement off his feet as if he were a play toy.

"Adam is happy! Adam is happy! He is going with Clement!"

"That's enough! Put me down, Adam!" Clement hollered.

Olaf and Osment, who had been watching them, broke out into a fit of laughter, which caused Adam to join them in their mirth. He gently set Clement back down and followed him outside.

Clement had strapped his dagger onto his belt, under his cloak. Lightly armed, they quietly headed down the cobbled street.

"Look! Look! The seagulls! Clement, look!"

Adam rushed in among them wanting to play. They quickly dispersed, squawking loudly, as they took to the evening sky. Clement smiled as he watched Adam raising his arms, trying in vain to call them back. They moved along, leaving the cobbled road and turning onto a small narrow lane lined with dirty clapboard houses where fishermen dwelled. They were near the end of the lane when two men dressed in shabby dark cloaks and moth-eaten wool caps stepped out from behind stacked barrels in front of the cooper's shop. One was a young man, tall and broad at the shoulders. His companion was shorter, older and grizzled looking.

"Step out of my way!" Clement ordered.

The two ruffians glanced at one another. The older one, toothless, was grinning maliciously. At nearly the same time, both men pulled daggers from beneath their cloaks.

"Clement de la Haye! If ye know what is good fer yuh, ye better come wid us!"

Chapter 5

nly the older man spoke. The young one stood expressionless with a piece of stringy fish caught in his unkempt black beard.

"I'd throw that dagger of yours on the ground in front of ye, boy, before ye hurt yourself with it. Try to use it and I will cut ye head off with it."

Clement had pulled his weapon out and stood defiantly, glaring at the two men who blocked his path. Adam stood next to him, wearing a confused expression. His small eyes darted back and forth between the two men.

"What do you want?" Clement asked. "If you do not remove yourself from our presence, you will face dire consequences."

The older man waved his dagger in front of him as if he were carving an imaginary slab of meat.

"Such brave words coming from a little boy! Ye not much of a threat without that bow of yours, ye skinny little runt!"

He tapped his younger companion on the arm with the tip of his dagger and then waved it again in Clement's direction.

"Looks like this boy is going to have his throat cut before Sven has a chance to pluck his fingernails out one by one."

Adam was listening to the threatening tone of the two men and, although he was still confused as to why they were blocking their path, he knew enough. They meant to harm his friend and that simply was not going to happen with him by Clement's side.

"Clement! Clement! You want to hurt Clement!"

"Shut your mouth, ye simple-minded brute!" the older man said angrily. "Where did ye find this idiot?" he asked, addressing Clement.

Clement felt his blood boiling and gripped his dagger so tightly his knuckles were turning white.

"How dare you insult my friend! I will have both of you flogged and drummed out of town for that remark! Now step aside! You are detaining a servant of the king!"

"King Henry? He is not my king. Nor is he yours!" the older man said, edging closer toward his prey. "Now come with us before ye get hurt, unless ye choose death."

He advanced toward Clement, who cautiously started to back off. The man was nearly a head taller than the boy and much heavier. Clement, however, was much quicker. When the brute grabbed at Clement's cloak, Clement slashed at him with his dagger and cut a wide gash across the back of the attacker's hand. Meanwhile, the younger brute rushed toward Adam with his dagger but immediately regretted the decision. The dagger plunged forward and ended up slicing a huge opening in the space between Adam's broad shoulder and his elbow, barely nicking his skin. Adam, realizing the man was trying to hurt him, effortlessly picked him up and hurled him into the empty cooper's barrels, which went scattering in all directions. The man slowly gained his feet and saw the big lubberly boy advancing toward him with his arms outstretched, a look of rage on his face. He immediately took the prudent course of action and fled down the lane as fast as his legs could carry him. Adam saw Clement grappling with the older man. The man had grabbed onto the young count's cloak with one hand while attempting to slash at him with the dagger. Clement kept dodging the blade and, at one point, sliced another wound across the man's neck. He screamed and immediately let go of the boy's cloak to instinctively reach for his bleeding neck. His hand was covered with blood and, had the cut been a little deeper, it would have almost certainly been fatal. Clement advanced again with his dagger raised and the man, realizing that he had totally underestimated the skill of the boy, attempted to retreat but ended up running into a human wall.

"You hurt Clement!"

Adam lifted him up over his head as if he were a log and, once again, a man was flying through the air. He tumbled over a barrel and landed on his back with a sickening thud. Adam rushed over toward the fallen man with his arms outstretched, ready to grab him again.

"You are a mean man! You hurt Clement!"

"Adam! No! That's enough!" Clement said, rushing over to the fallen brute who was still on his back, groaning miserably. Adam stopped and lowered his arms, watching Clement who was hovering over his defeated foe poised to strike the life out of him with his dagger should he attempt to fight. The man's eyes were glossy and a trickle of blood was running out of his nose onto his bushy moustache.

"I have you beaten, foe! Do you yield?" Clement asked, pressing the point of his sharp dagger up to the fallen man's neck.

"Aye…" The man said, spitting out a mouthful of blood. "I yield, sire."

"Who are you? And why did you attack us? How do you know Sven?"

The man hesitated to speak.

"Speak, wretch! Did Sven send you?"

"Aye, Sven plans to kill ye…and that…that young lass of yours."

Clement's eyes narrowed. He pursed his lips angrily, pressing the blade against the man's cheek.

"Is Sven here in Harfleur? Don't lie to me!"

The beaten man shook his head fearfully, looking beyond the diminutive Clement to the imposing form of Adam standing behind him. He wiped his nose with the back of his hand, leaving a streak of blood on it.

"Nay… he is not…but he will be."

"I should gouge your eyes out. But I do not do those sorts of vile things. You can take a message back to my wicked uncle, Sven. You tell him that Clement de la Haye fears him not and if he should attempt to take my life by nefarious means again, why not try to do it himself?"

Clement stood and replaced his dagger in its sheath. He recovered both of his enemy's blades and smiled at his bloodied foe.

"I hope he paid you well, scoundrel. I'll be keeping these," the boy said, inspecting the quality of his two trophies. He handed them to Adam to carry with instructions that they were not toys.

"Come, Adam. Let us leave this fool before the buzzards start to encircle him."

Adam gave the man one last glance and shook his fist at him.

"That'll...that'll teach you, bad man!"

The bloodied assassin sat up and watched them leave with relief. A small crowd of fishermen and their families had gathered around the curious scene.

Clement and Adam arrived at the White Gull to find two of the three captains and Trousett already seated around a table. Only Sir William had not yet arrived. A pot of ale with stone mugs, a freshly baked loaf of potato bread, and large slabs of butter on a pewter tray awaited them. Clement had not had a morsel of food since morning and was famished. They watched him approach and were shocked at his disheveled appearance. There was a streak of dried blood on his face and his cloak was torn on his left arm from where his foe's dagger had sliced through it, barely missing muscle. He sat down next to Trousett. Adam handed him the confiscated daggers.

"The spoils of battle, gentlemen," he said, placing them down on the table in front of him.

"What the devil has happened to you, sire?" Trousett asked with astonishment. "'Tis blood on your face."

Clement shrugged. "Adam and I were set upon by a couple of fiends sent by my uncle Sven. We handled them with ease."

"But...but the blood?"

"Tis not my blood, Trousett, but the blood of my enemy."

Clement snapped his fingers, then held up his arm and waved to get the innkeepers attention. A plump woman with a saggy chin hustled over to the table, carrying a cloth.

"Will you fetch me a basin with water so I may wash my face?"

"Yes, sire, of course," she said, noticing the blood on his face, "but perhaps you might want to come back to the kitchen. I can wash ye myself, sire."

"I thank thee, missus,"

A few minutes later, he felt refreshed and by the time he arrived back at the table, Sir William was there. His eyes were stone cold. Clement sat across from him and helped himself to a hunk of bread. The two captains that he had not formerly met, were sitting on either side of Sir William. Neither said a word to him as they waited to be formerly introduced.

"Well, forgive my rudeness, gentlemen. I am famished!" Clement said, over a mouthful of bread, "I am Clement, count de la Haye, if you are not aware by now."

The younger of the two men leaned forward.

"The king speaks highly of you, sire. Allow me to introduce myself. I am Ceres, at your service."

The Greek stood up and bowed. He was a tall man with narrow features and bronzed skin. His raven black beard was neatly trimmed and he had a pleasant air about him that Clement immediately liked. The other man remained seated. He was older than Ceres, stocky, with a hooked nose and a large mole above his left eye. His beard was speckled with grey, but he seemed to be in fit condition. He was the only one at the table not wearing a cloak. He wore a loose-fitting tunic with his hairy arms exposed to the elements. The night was getting cool, but this did not seem to bother Roger de Montfort. He was more interested in what had just happened to his new boss, Clement de la Haye.

"You must be Roger de Montfort," Clement said extending his hand across the table. The recipient received it.

"And you must be the boy wonder the king reveres."

Clement frowned. "Well, I don't know about that, Sir Roger, but I do know a little bit about a few things, but...I am still young and perhaps can learn something from the men seated at this table. After all, we are all going on this journey together."

Sir Roger forced a smile. "You took those blades from your attackers. How?"

Clement shrugged. "It was quite easy wasn't it, Adam?" he asked, turning to his big friend.

Adam shook his head up and down in an exaggerated manner and placed a finger on his lips. He remembered what Clement had told him about speaking and following the instructions to the letter. Though Clement did not mean it to this extreme.

"They blocked our way and I ordered them out of our path. They refused and attacked. I fought the small one while Adam disposed of the big one. I am fairly handy with the blade, Sir Roger, and extremely fast."

"Did you dispatch them?" Sir Roger asked curiously.

"He did not, Sir Roger," Sir William chimed in.

Clement was puzzled and turned to his captain of the knar.

"How do you know this, Sir William?"

"Because I stumbled upon one of the wretches still sitting in the lane, all bloodied where you left him. When I asked one of the fishermen what had happened, he told me that a young nobleman and a giant had roughed him and his companion up. The description of the young nobleman fit you perfectly...thin, wiry, long yellow hair, wearing an expensive green cloak trimmed in gold. I took the liberty of finishing the job, sire."

"Pardon me?" Clement asked. He was clearly confused and thought that he might have misunderstood Sir William's statement.

"I dispatched him where he sat. Sent my blade clean through his heart. He shall bother you no more."

Sir William used a tone so callous Clement was shocked by what he had just heard.

"But...But I could have done that, Sir William, had I chosen to do so. But I had my man beat and he yielded to the threat of further punishment from my blade!" Clement exclaimed angrily.

"Only noblemen deserve the luxury of being spared by mercy. This man was from the lower order. He was an assassin sent to capture or kill you. Never turn your back on a man like this. He has no honor and will strike again when you least expect him. Now tell me...this other man... the big one, you let him go, too?"

Clement was appalled.

"He...he ran like a rushing wind."

Sir William cocked an eyebrow and glanced at Trousett, who was staring at the two blades.

"I underestimated you," Sir William said admiringly. "If you had slain that rogue, I would praise you too. Now, you know."

For a few seconds, there was an awkward silence. Clement thought about berating his subordinate but decided he would let the matter drop. He needed to move things along. He reached into his cloak and pulled out the rolled scroll that he had brought with him. Kneeling on the bench he spread it out on the table, using the stone mugs to hold it flat. The three captains all stood up and hovered over it as if it might reveal the location of the Holy Grail. Clement used one of his confiscated daggers as a pointer.

"This is where we sit today, enjoying the fraternal bonds of friendship."

He then ran the blade lightly over the map being careful not to slice it. He stopped at an elongated spot painted in light brown. He had delineated a fruit tree to emphasize the name written next to it.

"This is our destination."

"Vinland?" Ceres asked, his eyes focused squarely on the point. "I have never heard of it."

"Nor I," Sir Roger said. "How far is this place we seek?"

Clement looked up from the map, his face serious.

"At least a thousand leagues…maybe more."

There was dead silence broken only by Trousett clearing his throat.

Sir William's eyes became big. "A thousand leagues? Are you mad? The king did not say anything about this."

"No, he did not. He entrusted this information only to me and Trousett, and I now tell you as it is necessary for you to know. Gentlemen, this information is not to be revealed to anyone. I need your word as knights and men of honor that you will remain reticent as to the particulars of this voyage. People only need to know that we are on a trading mission to the wild lands of the Irish. Our true mission shall not be revealed."

"And what is our mission?" Sir William asked. "Since you seem to be the only one the king trusts!"

Clement detected a jealous tone to Sir William's voice, but ignored it.

"A fleet of ships led by a certain Sir Humphrey Rochford, left a port in Bretagne a fortnight ago. Intelligence reports say they are heading to Vinland via the Norse settlements to the west. Our mission is to find out what they are up to and why they are venturing to this far off land. Further instructions are contained in a sealed letter to be opened by me once we are a hundred leagues from the lands of the Irish. I suspect this letter contains further information regarding Sir Humphrey's motives and King Henry's plan to counter it. But this is only conjecture on my part."

Sir William slammed his fist down on the table causing the stone mugs to jump.

"Riches! Gold and silver! King Louis is behind this and King Henry knows it!"

Clement gave him a fixed look of astonishment.

"Perhaps, Sir William, but as I said, I will find out further instructions from our king when we are well out at sea."

"That is fine," Sir William replied condescendingly. "And just how are we to communicate on a voyage so long and how are we going to stay together as a fleet, traveling such a distance out of sight of land. This is totally absurd and a fool's errand."

"If we are beyond hailing distance," Clement explained, "I have created a simple means of communication via lantern signals."

Once again, Clement reached into his cloak. This time he pulled out four thin books. The parchment was protected by treated leather. Each book was identical. The pages illuminated with a complex series of colors and diagrams representing the codes they would use to communicate with one another through a series of instructions. For instance, a green flame could be made by mixing copper with the fuel.

"Did you create these, Sir Clement?" Sir William asked with astonishment, picking one up and perusing its contents.

"Yes. I had been working on it for my mariners when the king called me to Chinon Castle. It is not complete, but it will be helpful."

Sir Roger wagged his finger at Clement.

"What other surprises are you going to pull out of that cloak of yours, boy? The secret to finding eternal life perhaps?"

He laughed at his own joke. The attempt at humor caused even the rigid Sir William to crack a smile, but it was almost immediately replaced with a look of doubt.

"What is this ridiculousness?" he asked, pointing to an illustration on one of the back pages. On it, majestically painted in green, brown and white, was a monstrous looking creature entwining itself around a broken ship. He turned over the next page to see an image even more frightening. A monster with a massive bulbous head, its long sinewy arms entangled around the mast of a ship.

"This is foolishness!"

"Nay. Not foolishness, Sir William. Truth." Clement said, folding his arms on the table.

"Total rubbish. What is this thing called? How do you know it exists?"

"It is called a kraken, me lord," said a familiar voice behind Clement. "And I can assure ye that the lad here knows what he is talking about!"

"Gorm!" Clement screamed excitedly. He stood up and the two old friends embraced. One ancient and withered, the other young and lithe.

"Ye are taller, me lord! Just look at ye! Ye are almost my height!"

"Who is this?" Sir William demanded with arrogance, perceiving the low born status of Clement's friend.

"Oh...Oh... forgive me, gentlemen. This is my old friend, Gorm. He sailed with me on the Green Ship to the land of fire!"

Ceres stood up and offered Gorm his hand. The old man grasped it.

"A pleasure to meet you," Ceres said.

"Aye, me lord, the pleasure is mine,"

"Sit, Gorm, and have some ale with us!" Clement invited.

The old man sat next to Clement and eagerly tipped one of the stone mugs to his lips, without bothering to inquire as to its owner.

"We will miss you on this voyage, Gorm," Clement said dejectedly.

"Miss me? Nay, me lord. Ye won't miss me as I am going with thee!"

Clement appeared surprised. His mouth was partly opened, shocked by Gorm's bold statement.

"But...but you are too old, Gorm. You would never survive the voyage."

The old man chuckled, scratching his white whiskers and taking another draught of ale.

"Too old, ye say. Nay, me lord. From what I hear, ye are going to need all the experience ye can muster." He winked at Clement. "I wouldn't miss this voyage for anything in the world!"

Clement became excited, throwing his arm around Gorm's hunched shoulders and beaming with delight. Sir William was watching the scene with disgust.

"Then go with us you shall, my old friend. But this time, you will not sleep in the hold with the rest of the crew. We shall create a berth for you in the forecastle with Baldwin and Pierre! It shall be like old times! You will be my principal rudder man. Of course, you will delegate this task to the younger sailors."

"I thank thee, me lord, but if I go, I shall do me as much work as the next man. Me age is only a number, me lord. In fact, I cannot rightly say exactly how old I am. Three score? Maybe four?"

The two friends burst out laughing at the same time and Adam, not really comprehending the humor, joined them anyway. It was short lived as Sir William had seen enough.

"Are we going to proceed with this or not?" he interrupted.

Clement was still smiling, his youthful exuberance irritating William de Bayeux.

"I am sorry gentlemen, of course, but you see it has been nearly a year since I have seen Gorm, and we are good friends."

"That is nice to hear, but back to this map of yours, Sir Clement," Sir William replied snidely. "How do you know it is authentic? I have never heard of these lands beyond the area you have marked Greenland. What is this place, for instance? The darkened region you have labeled Markland."

Clement became serious again.

"I have been studying the Norse scrolls and have in my possession other scrolls of ancient origin that talk about a large continent many miles to the west of Greenland. It is said to be a land of abundance. Great mountains and primeval virgin forests untouched by man. It is near here we shall find the place known as Vinland, which is said to contain a great bay with a snake like protruding arm of land that curves like the letter C."

"How do you know for sure?" Sir Roger asked, interrupting Sir William, who was about to ask the same question.

"Because gentlemen...there are too many references to it. Believe me when I say this. It is there and we shall find it!"

Sir William was dubiously shaking his head and seemed ready to start plucking the grey hairs from his beard.

"I have been told the sea continues on until it drops off the edge of the world. Ships have reported this phenomenon. How do you know we will reach this land you call Markland before we fall into the abyss!"

Clement was smirking.

"The earth is not flat, Sir William. It is round. If we sail due west at the same latitude, we will eventually reach the spot in which we started."

"Your confidence in this regard is much stronger than mine, young man. How do you know this for fact?"

"It is simple science and logic," Clement said. "Look up at the stars on a clear night. They are round, as is the moon and the sun. When there is an eclipse, this proves it!"

"An eclipse?"

"Yes, Sir William, an eclipse is when the moon passes across the solar disk of the sun. It is not God's wrath as some would have it, but simple Science! When you look at the horizon on the shore and see a sail, you only see the top of it at first and as it nears the shore, you see more and more of it until all of it comes into view. This is caused by the curvature of the earth. Now do you see it?"

Sir William leaned forward with piercing eyes.

"What I see is a vile case of heresy if you are not careful, Sir Clement,"

The boy smiled with a look of condescending intellectual superiority, but Sir William deserved it. He sat there festering in his ignorance and Clement could not help but feel a certain loathing for him.

"Call it what you will, Sir William. Time will prove me right. I can assure you there is no danger of sailing off the edge of the world."

Ceres was busy studying Clement's book and the boy realized here at least was one man who possessed a keen open mind. It was then that Gorm chimed in, directing his warning at Sir William with aged and wizened, penetrating eyes.

"Ye all would be best served to heed and study the book the boy hath given thee. The ocean is a dangerous place. I myself shall not return to me native land once I set forth, but my eyes will see the new one before I pass. If ye do not heed thy warnings ye shall not see it. Remember this, or the ocean will claim ye!"

Chapter 6

It was a cold windy day when the fleet pulled anchor. The sky was full of puffy white clouds and the gulls squawked alongside the ships as men unfurled the sails and manned the oars. A large crowd had gathered along the quay. Vendors selling fish and pork lined the docks, as little children ran along getting in a last glimpse of the Green Ship as it slowly pulled away. The crowd cheered as the young fleet admiral climbed to the crow's nest on the mast, doffed his cap and let the wind blow his long yellow locks across his face. Clement had set a target on the dock and a prearranged signal from the harbor master let him know it was safe to let an arrow fly. The small children on the dock were ready. Clement pulled back his string and let it fly. His aim, coming with no surprise, was true and accurate, hitting the bullseye dead center despite the wind. The children rushed forward and there was a scramble to see who would claim it. A little toe-headed boy leaped around a big freckled red head and swiftly pulled the arrow from its mark, claiming his prize. The men cheered from the decks of the ships as the boy was lifted onto the shoulders of a man for everyone to see as the crowd gathered around them. Clement pointed at the boy and waved. Dagena was standing on a crate, leaning over the railing and throwing coins to the people standing on the quay, but as the ship receded further away, some landed in the water. In the scramble to retrieve them, a scuffle ensued and a portly man, wearing a baker's apron, ended up doing a belly flop into the water, which caused a great deal of laughter from the people on the ships. They could see the embarrassed baker's wet head bobbing up and down in the water.

Clement descended the rope ladder and joined Dagena and Olaf on the deck. Gorm was given the honor of moving the ship away from the harbor and, in the week leading up to the departure, had become somewhat of a celebrity, sitting on the dock telling stories from his years at sea and holding the young children spellbound by his often-exaggerated exploits and adventures. The last vessel to depart was the Brown Ship, captained by Sir William. It seemed intentionally to trail the others. Clement watched the people standing on the quay at Harfleur until they became mere specks and, finally, the whole scene blended into the shoreline. Eventually, the land became a dark hazy mass until finally it could be seen no more. They were all alone, on the ocean. Only themselves. Clement felt a sense of foreboding doom and began to doubt himself the further his fleet left the land behind them. His plan was to skirt the coast of Normandy and then sail northwest into the Celtic sea toward the wild lands of the Irish. He planned to trade with them and fill his casks with fresh water and victuals. He knew it would be uncertain where he would again be able to resupply. West of Ireland, he planned on following a certain latitude that would take him to the Norse settlements in Greenland. It was doubtful he could trade for supplies there and might even be met with hostility. After this, he was sailing into the unknown. Vinland was somewhere to the west, but where? He knew not, but he was confident he would run into something. Strange lands lay to the west and unexplored tracts of land. Were there people who lived in these places? Or were they devoid of human habitation? Perhaps strange beasts roamed these lands, or maybe there was nothing at all. A barren landscape with no life like the large sand deserts of the east.

Nearly noon, Clement felt the cool wind on his back and decided to take an altitude reading with his astrolabe. He planned to perform this task at least once a day in order to adjust his direction of travel. He kept a log in a book, which he kept with his other books, on a small shelf in the sterncastle. He had brought a few invaluable books that might help him along the way, including Ptolemy's *Almagest* and *Geography* along with his treasured *Book of Optics* by the Arab scholar Ibn al-Haytham.

Although he was surrounded by people with seafaring experience, he felt alone in the knowledge that, without him, they would become terribly lost.

As far as he knew, the only other person on the voyage who could take a latitude reading was Ceres. Sir William and Sir Roger were excellent navigators as to the control of their vessels, and both could read a map with some skill, but neither possessed the aptitude for taking astronomical measurements or working out equations and formulas. To his knowledge, only he possessed these skills. They would be in trouble if he were somehow incapacitated. He had given Ceres his spare astrolabe in case the Green Ship should founder. At least he would be able to keep them at the same latitude, or in a position where they might be able to recover their bearings. Trousett could navigate and read a map, but he too lacked the skills necessary to read an astrolabe, though he was learning.

When he was done taking his reading, he recorded it and returned the logbook to the cabin, where he found Dagena and Alice brewing some chicory water.

"I sure do wish we had some of those beans from Kaldi we had last time we sailed on the Green Ship," Clement said.

Dagena smiled. "Perhaps we will find some in this new land we seek. We don't know what we shall discover!"

He sat down at the table. Dagena handed him a mug of chicory water. The only light in the castle came from an oil lamp and a small window above the fire pit. The window had a hatch which could be snapped into place in case of inclement weather. Baldwin had thought of everything. As Clement was perusing one of his maps, Alice suddenly flew out of the sterncastle and, within a few seconds, she was at the rail heaving into the choppy sea. Dagena followed her friend and tried to console her.

"What the devil! I've never been so sick, Dagena."

"You will recover…come, let me help you back into the cabin."

Alice let her friend and former foe assist her back into the sterncastle. Crawling into her bunk she felt like retching again, but Dagena placed a cold wet cloth on her head and she began to feel a little better.

"Maybe this was a mistake, Dagena," Alice mumbled.

"I was sick the first time I went to sea, Alice. Not everyone can be as lucky as Clement and Olaf and never once feel a tinge of sickness." Olaf had entered the castle with Pierre.

"What is wrong?"

"What do you think is wrong, Olaf," Clement said, not even bothering to look up from his map. "Alice is sick. So is Adam. He is making his bed in your bunk right now. I hope you don't mind."

"My bunk?" Olaf was appalled. "Why didn't you put him in yours?"

Clement looked up at his friend with a devilish grin.

"Because he wanted to sleep in your bunk."

"Well...I hope he doesn't retch in it," Olaf said, with a look of disgust.

"He can barely fit in it Olaf. His legs hang off the sides."

"I'm going to check on Alice."

He started toward her small berth but Dagena emerged from behind the curtain. She had a snarl on her face.

"You will do nothing of the kind. Do you think she wants you to see her in this condition? She has too much dignity for that. Get out of here."

She then turned to Clement. "That goes for you too...out! Both of you, while I tend to the sick!"

She shuffled over to where Clement was sitting. He started to rise and she began pushing him.

"Out!"

"But I'm the fleet admiral, Dagena. You can't throw me out of my own headquarters," he said, winking at Olaf.

Her oval eyes narrowed. "I certainly can!"

Clement leaped over the bench and Dagena, wielding a broom, chased both boys out of the sterncastle and slammed the door behind them. Once out in the open air, they both began laughing. They immediately noticed Pierre leaning over the starboard rail. His face ashen and, despite the coolness of the day, he had broken out into a cold sweat.

"You too?" Clement asked.

The Frenchman turned to the boy with glossy eyes.

"Oh, sire...I am miserable."

Clement shook his head and motioned with his thumb toward the sterncastle.

"Dagena will fix you up, Pierre."

As Pierre was staggering toward what he hoped was a cure for his hellish condition, Olaf called to him.

"Pierre, Clement's bunk is available! I believe his pillow has been fluffed!"

Clement cringed.

"Thanks, Olaf!"

Once again, the two friends fed off each other's laughter. This attracted Gorm, who came over and joined them at the rail.

"Ah, such a lovely breeze coming off the channel. I am home again, upon the seas!"

"Others onboard this boat would beg to differ with you, Gorm," Clement replied.

Gorm winked. "Aye, half the crew be below deck sick to their rotten stomachs. Gorging on halibut the night before departure was not the best idea, but ye live and ye learn, sire. Poor Jacques, ye giant friend is down below tending to the sick. As big and mean as he looks, he is as kind and compassionate as a nun."

"I had halibut last evening and it didn't affect me, Gorm," Olaf said, placing his hand on his stomach as if he were waiting for a twinge of nausea.

Gorm chuckled. "Ye a Dane like me, boy. The Dane is born to the sea."

"Well, I'm half a Dane," Clement said, trying to make sense of Gorm's unscientific logic.

"Ye Normans are born to it also, sire," Gorm added.

"Well, I am a descendent of Rollo," Clement boasted. "I've never been sick at sea."

Gorm's weary eyes scanned the horizon as the Green Ship bobbed effortlessly over the rough sea.

"Gorm, have you ever been to Hibernia?" Clement asked curiously.

"Aye, sire, numerous times. The land is rugged but green and lovely. The people are a wild boisterous lot. Ye will not find a book among them, sire. They are clannish and when ye trade with them, ye need to have eyes behind ye head!"

"Can you speak their language, Gorm?" Olaf asked.

"Aye, I lived among them for near a year and learned a little of their tongue. It is a course, hard language, but ye get to know it well when ye live among them. It has been a few years since I have been there, but there is a king, a fierce man named Mac Lochlainn. It would be wise to steer clear of him, sire."

Clement frowned. "And why is that? I bring good will from our king along with a message for this Mac Lochlainn. As the king's ambassador and a nobleman, he shall receive me with the dignity my title deserves."

"I warn ye, sire. The man has two faces. One he shows, the other he hides."

"I thank thee for the warning, Gorm, but I am just a messenger. I would like you to come with me as part of the landing party," Clement said. "I am learned in many tongues, but the speech of the Irish I know not."

"Then I shall translate for you, sire, but we have many days before we arrive there. I shall teach ye some words so ye can exchange pleasantries with them."

The days passed with no remarkable incidents taking place aboard the vessels, which managed to keep relatively close together. They used the signals Clement had created to communicate with one another. The Brown Ship kept its distance from the others, but still managed to keep in contact with the other three. Clement wondered if this was the intentional rebellious spirit of its captain, or if it merely had trouble keeping up with the rest of the fleet. They passed into the Irish Sea. Clement had been here before and recognized many of the landmarks as they sailed close to the Scottish coast. At one point, they were so close they could see people standing along the shore watching the fleet pass.

A few days later, they turned west, rounding the Irish coast. It was a rocky shoreline with a few beaches and basaltic cliffs that towered above them. To their north, they passed a small island which Clement had not seen on his previous voyage two years earlier. He studied it carefully through his glass and added it to his globe. It was a misty morning but the lookout in the crow's nest was the first to see it.

"Castle! High on the bluff!"

Clement rushed to the port rail, glass in hand. A crowd had gathered around him, wondering what he would do. Peering through the mist he could see only the top of the castle. The rest was enveloped by a glistening fog fighting with the sunlight for dominance in the early dawn.

"It be Dunseverick Castle, me lord," Gorm stated confidently. "'Tis seat of the O'Kanes. Ye will find this Mac Lochlainn near here, or within a few days.

"Let us anchor in the bay and I will send a messenger to fetch this king of Ireland," Clement said suddenly.

"He will not come to ye. Ye will have to go to him, me lord," Gorm said.

"We will see," Clement replied.

The vessels anchored in the bay. Clement noticed a crowd had gathered on the beach. Men armed with bows and other weapons stood anxiously wondering who had arrived unexpectedly on their coast. Clement signaled to the other ships in his fleet to anchor farther off the shore as to alleviate some of the anxiety among the throng on the beach. He did not want them to misread his intent. Clement stuffed the king's letter to Mac Lochlainn in his cloak and ordered the skiff be readied.

"Sire, I highly recommend you let me or someone else go ashore first," Pierre stated with concern.

Clement was nervously chewing on his lower lip.

"No, Pierre. My instructions from the king were explicit. I am going ashore with a few men to row me and that is the end of it."

Trousett appeared next to him.

"As the king's agent, I am going with you."

The boy looked at him suspiciously.

"Trousett, I agreed you could travel with me on the Green Ship because the king insisted on it, but besides me, only you have the navigation skills necessary to bring this ship where it needs to go. You shall remain on board."

The king's cartographer started to argue the point when Clement noticed Olaf boarding the skiff, his blade tucked neatly into his scabbard. A few strong rowers, including Jacques, had also climbed in beside Olaf. The Danish boy had a smile on his face and Clement merely rolled his eyes. Osment, too, was preparing to board, along with Dagena and Alice, but Clement would have none of this.

"Out, all of you!"

"You once saved my skin, Clement," Osment said. "The least I can do is watch your back."

"Sorry, Osment. But I must go alone. You need to stay here. As second in rank, and the only other person of noble birth on this vessel, you are now temporary captain of the Green Ship."

His friend hesitated but given such a responsibility, reluctantly decided to obey Clement's order. Dagena had quickly returned to the sterncastle for something. Clement decided it was now or never, so, after Gorm climbed in next to Olaf, he jumped aboard and ordered the skiff lowered. By the time Dagena returned to the rail, the skiff was in the water. She angrily shook her fist in the air.

"Clement, just wait until you come back on board!"

She threw a walnut at him but the throw was misaimed and the nut struck Olaf on the cheek.

"Ow! Dagena, what did I do to you?"

"That was not meant for you, Olaf! But the next one will be if something happens to Clement!"

Clement broke out into a fit of laughter. This time the walnut hit its mark, ricocheting off his shoulder and landing in Gorm's lap.

"Ah! Me thinks I'll have a tasty treat," Gorm said, examining the nut.

The bit of humor caused everyone in the skiff, including the rowers, to laugh. Clement kneeled on the bow of the small boat, watching the shoreline creep closer. Surprisingly, he was not a bit nervous. Besides Jacques and the other three rowers, only he, Olaf and Gorm were coming ashore. Surely this small force, which included two teenage boys and an old man, could not possibly be a threat to the three dozen or so armed men who had gathered on the beach. As they came closer, Clement noticed one of them seemed to stand out among the others. A fierce looking brute with long flowing red hair, wearing a dark wool cloak was standing a few yards in front of the rest of the men. His legs were bare except for a pair of sandals strapped halfway up the calf in the manner of the Romans of yore. There was a boy about Clement's age standing next to him. A tough looking sod, every feature in miniature of the brute. Clement correctly deduced this was the man's son, whoever he might be.

Clement felt the bottom of the skiff scraping sand and he leaped into the surf, knee deep, followed by Olaf. Almost immediately, they were surrounded by the fierce looking brute's men who had drawn their swords and formed a circle around them. The brutish looking man was drawn to Jacques. Being by far the largest of the invaders, he was naturally assumed to be their leader. The red-haired man was attempting to interrogate Jacques in the Gaelic tongue, which to everyone but Gorm seemed wholly unintelligible. Clement found himself face to face with the boy whom he had seen on the shore. The Irish lad was staring at him with a fierce look, as if he were itching to plunge his blade into the Norman boy's heart at the first sign from his father. The two boys were nearly the same height but the Irish lad was much stockier, and Clement realized if they were to go toe to toe, he would have to outwit this boy using speed and brain power.

Clement attempted to turn and say something to the Gaelic leader but when he did, the boy in front of him grabbed him by the front of his cloak and held a dagger to his neck. Olaf started to draw his sword and come to Clement's aid but his arms were immediately pinioned by two stout men, who quickly disarmed him. Things were about to escalate when suddenly Gorm, who was being ignored, let out a flurry of curses in the Gaelic tongue, which arrested all movement. For a few seconds, there was silence and then the red-haired brute turned to Gorm and started to laugh. Gorm was holding up his well weathered hands and began talking to the man in a mixture of Gaelic and Norman.

"So, you are Normans?" the Gaelic leader asked, astonishingly in perfect Norman. "Why didn't you say so? We thought you were Norse."

"Aye, sir. I be a Dane by birth," Gorm said, "but sail under a Norman flag."

"And you...old man...the leader?"

Gorm bowed. "No, sire. I am but a humble sailor, skilled in the language of your culture."

"I am the admiral of this fleet!" Clement interrupted. "Now please order this boy to lower his blade. It feels too hot against my neck, and I think too highly of my neck to possibly lose it."

"Tieg! Release him!"

The boy reluctantly lowered his blade, but his piercing green eyes remained fixed on Clement as if he were disappointed, he did not get to cut him.

Tieg's father approached Clement, studying him carefully.

"You are the leader of this fleet of ships? A mere boy?"

Clement nodded. "I am Clement, Count de la Haye, son of Hugo. This is my fleet. I have arrived on your shore for two reasons. I seek an audience with the king known as Mac Lochlainn. But first, who is it I address? Tieg's father, perhaps?" Clement asked sarcastically, glancing at Tieg with contempt.

The man grinned.

"Aye, I am Tieg's father. My name is Padraig O'Kane, and if it is Mac Lochlainn you seek, you have arrived at the right time. I expect him on this very night."

Clement glanced over at Olaf, who had been released and had his sword returned. Jacques was standing with the other three rowers, strong Norman men loyal to Clement, who were watching their hosts suspiciously.

"Paidraig O'Kane, we have journeyed far and wish to top off our water supply."

Padraig nodded. "There is a spring that flows from the rocks."

He whistled and pointed to a short stout man wearing a dirty white tunic. The man approached hastily and said something in Gaelic.

"Rory will show you where it is."

Clement turned to Jacques and the three sailors.

"Jacques, can you see to it?"

"Yes, sire, consider it done, but it shall take some time. Being no quay to dock we will have to load the barrels on rafts and tow them."

"Thank you, Jacques. Have Osment signal to the rest of the fleet. We will do one vessel at a time."

Clement turned to his host, who was studying him carefully.

"I don't understand," Padraig said mystified.

"What is it you don't understand, Padraig O'Kane?" Clement asked seriously.

"How is it a boy is given the command of such a fleet as this? How old are you? Twelve?"

"I am fourteen. My good friend Olaf, is fifteen and my other good friend, Gorm, is...well he might be sixty or eighty, but age is merely a number."

"Then you are my son's age," Padraig said, pointing at Tieg, who was standing off to the side with a perturbed look, listening.

"The ship you see anchored closest to the shore is my own," Clement stated. "The rest belong to King Henry. It is he who is responsible for us landing on your shore, but it is Mac Lochlainn whom I seek. I have a message to impart to him from my king."

Padraig cocked a cynical eye. He wetted his lips and peered out at the quartet of vessels anchored in his bay.

"That is a marvelous looking specimen," he said admiringly, gesturing toward the Green Ship. "I would give you a chest full of silver for it, Clement de la Haye."

"And I would not sell it, Padraig O'Kane, but tell me...how do you speak our language?"

"I learned from a countryman, who landed on our shores during the time of the first King Henry. I was but a youth then. I traveled with him to Normandy and lived for half a dozen years among your people before returning to my native land. My wife, God rest her soul, hailed from that land of plenty."

Padraig was looking beyond Clement toward the Green Ship and espied Dagena and Alice leaning on the rail.

"You have women on board your vessel, Clement de la Haye?"

Clement squinted into the morning sunlight. The bright rays caused the calm water of the bay to sparkle.

"Aye, the Lady Dagena and the Lady Alice."

"Of good breeding?" Padraig asked rudely.

Clement's head turned sharply toward his host.

"Explain yourself, sir?"

"Are they of noble blood?"

"Yes," he lied, thinking of Dagena. He almost immediately regretted divulging this to the Irishman. There was something about him he did not trust. What if he had ill intent? He trusted that Osment and Pierre would post a strong guard on the vessel and see to its security, but he was still concerned. Padraig O'Kane could muster hundreds of men if he were so inclined. What if he decided to make a night attack on the ship?

"Well, then! Let us tarry on this shore no longer, Clement de la Haye. It is not often we have amiable guests not concerned with plunder."

He turned to one of his trusted men and whispered something in his ear. Clement walked with his host. Olaf and Gorm followed. Tieg and a few of Padraig's men took up the rear at a distance. They scaled a narrow path, lined by rocks and thick brambles, that led up the cliff to the castle.

Dunseverick castle was a small edifice. It was not as grand as some of the French and Norman castles, but, nevertheless, stood out, and was an impressive sight. It dominated the countryside, sitting high on the bluff with its stone walls and spacious courtyard and stable. By the time they had climbed to the top, Gorm was out of breath and had to be assisted by Olaf. Clement looked out into the bay and could see the anchored ships. He recognized Jacque's massive form, looking ridiculously small in the skiff, but Dagena and Alice had disappeared from view. He wondered what they were doing. Padraig led them into the great hall and whistled to a servant, who seemingly appeared out of nowhere.

"Bring us some mead!"

They sat down on crude-built benches around a table, generations old. The walls of the castle were darkened by soot. The whole place seemed to reek of scorched wood. Clement noticed the hall was sparsely decorated when compared to most of the castles he had seen over the course of his short life. He wondered if this was the way with the Irish or, perhaps, Padraig O'Kane was a man of stature and not wealth.

"So, what is it you wish to tell Mac Lochlainn?" Padraig asked inquisitively, his green eyes twitching.

"What I have to say is for Mac Lochlainn's ears only," Clement said, folding his hands on the table in front of him. He was reluctant to tell his host about the letter in his cloak for fear Padraig would attempt to gain it by force. He had no way of knowing what kind of relationship the two men had and did not wish to fan the flames of the fire if one should be burning between the two.

"I am merely a messenger, Padraig O'Kane. I was given firm instructions from my king and I intend on carrying them out. If Mac Lochlainn wishes to share the message with you, then that is for him to decide."

Padraig leaned forward, just as the servant returned with a tray containing five mugs of mead. Clement was not particularly fond of this beverage but decided to be polite and sample it. Tieg, who had been standing behind his father with his arms folded, sat down across from Olaf, who was studying him suspiciously.

"You speak boldly and with confidence for one so young," Padraig said. "Almost as if you were a knight."

"He is a knight," Olaf said, interrupting him. "His archery skills are second to none."

A hint of a smile crossed the Gaelic chieftain's ruddy face. "How are his wrestling skills?"

Olaf glanced at Clement, who had a perturbed look on his face.

"Well, he is a fair fighter, as am I, Padraig O'Kane."

"Then I suggest some entertainment for a prize," Padraig said coldly, turning to Clement. "You will fight Tieg. If Tieg wins, you will divulge the reason for your visit to me before Mac Lochlainn arrives. Oh, and you have arrived at a most opportune time. The matches of the best wrestlers in the kingdom will be held tonight, as well as the challenge for top archer. But you and Tieg shall have your own private match before our king arrives."

"And if I win?" Clement asked, aware of Tieg's penetrating gaze.

"If you win?" Padraig seemed confused by Clement's question. "But you won't win, Clement de la Haye."

"Let me understand something," Clement said forcefully. "As the challenged party, I get to choose the nature of the contest."

Padraig grinned, showing his rotting yellow teeth.

"That may be how it works in Normandy, Clement de la Haye, but you are not in Normandy."

"I will fight Tieg," Olaf interjected.

Padraig shrugged. "I might agree to that, Dane!"

Clement reluctantly took a sip of his mead. He wanted to spit in Padraig's face, but decided prudently he would play his game. Whatever was going on between O'Kane and Mac Lochlainn was no concern of his, but Padraig must have some idea what King Henry's message might contain.

"You haven't answered my question, Padraig O'Kane," Clement muttered. "What will my prize be?"

Padraig's eyes narrowed and he leaned across the table.

"Your freedom, if you must know!"

He pounded his fist on the table, causing Clement to jump back in surprise. Olaf instinctively placed his hand on the pommel of his sword.

"You insult me!" Clement exclaimed angrily. "I came here to deliver a message from my king and you threaten me?"

Padraig folded his arms and began playing with his thick red beard, a habit he practiced when he was thinking.

"I do not threaten you, Clement de la Haye. I merely need to know what intelligence you possess before it is divulged to my king. You are proving to be difficult."

Padraig motioned for Rory to approach. He then whispered in his ear.

"Let the garrison and village know there will be a special contest held at the games in the courtyard, an hour before dusk. This will provide plenty of time to divulge the information I want from the boy count before our king arrives."

Chapter 7

Word of the upcoming special match spread like wildfire. Although no one had ever heard of the Norman count known as Clement de la Haye, people imagined him to be a fierce knight with bulging muscles and a glimmering sword made in heaven. They had gathered on the cliffs to admire the fleet of ships anchored in the bay. Any person who could gather a quartet of impressive vessels such as these, and sail them from the coast of Normandy, must be someone to be reckoned with. Soon, however, it became known that Clement de la Haye was a mere lad of fourteen, slight of build, and certainly not a match for any of the wild warriors Padraig O'Kane could match against him.

Clement stood on the allure overlooking the courtyard. It was here the games were to take place within the hour. Olaf and Gorm were standing with him, very pensive and worried about the situation. Jacques was still leading the effort to replenish the water but Padraig O'Kane had refused to negotiate with Clement regarding the trade that he had counted on to take place. Clement hoped to be able to trade wine and linen for salted pork, which he had not been able to find in abundance in Normandy due to a swine sickness. People were starting to congregate in the courtyard, which was shaped like a small oval bowl. It had the appearance of a festive gathering. Families were arriving by the dozens, claiming prime spots close to the perimeter. The prime seats, of course, were reserved for the family of Padraig O'Kane and some of the wealthier people in the village, including the high sheriff, who was there to make certain the contests were fair.

"You don't have to fight him," Olaf said nervously. "I will fight him. You only need to best him with your bow."

Clement was rubbing his chin and thinking. He had barely heard his friend's remarks. It was then he saw something that made his heart start to beat rapidly in his chest.

"Dagena!"

Olaf and Gorm saw her about the same time. She was with Alice and William de Bayeux. They were being led to the prime seats in a large wooden pavilion with a shingled slanted roof. Tables had been set up with refreshments for the well to do people watching the games. Padraig had called for the tournament weeks before and some of the best archers and fighters from northern Hibernia were planning on attending. Clement clenched his fists and felt a rage boiling up inside.

"They tricked us!" he shouted.

"They must have told them you requested their presence on the shore or Osment would not have let them go," Olaf said angrily. "Jacques must have told them all was well, going back and forth with no restrictions as he is doing. How was he to know?"

Clement looked up at the sky. He slammed his fist into the palm of his hand.

"I need my bow, Olaf."

"What are you going to do?"

The young count smiled. "I am going to show them what a skilled archer can do when he is upset!"

Gorm was pacing back and forth on the allure, looking grave and ill.

"I do not trust this Padraig O'Kane, me lord," he said in a low voice, "But this man Mac Lochlainn who ye seek is even more treacherous. Though I have never met him, I have seen him from afar and this O'Kane reminds me of him. He played me captain dirty and we barely left these shores alive near a score of years ago."

Clement was about to turn down the stairs leading to the hall when Tieg suddenly appeared from the dark recess of the stairway. He was smirking and Clement could plainly see why. He was holding his bow and quiver.

"That is mine! Give it here!" Clement ordered.

Tieg willingly handed it over and Clement studied it carefully to see if it had suffered any ill effects.

"How did you get this?" Clement demanded.

The Irish boy shrugged.

"That young lass with the bright red hair brought it in the boat," Tieg replied honestly. "She was told that there was to be a shooting match and that one of the contestants was to be the boy count of la Haye. Well, there it is."

Clement was still examining his well-constructed bow. It was a brand new one made from yew, skillfully honed by his hands.

"It is a small bow but I hear ye are quite good with it," Tieg stated, frankly. "But are ye as good as Claude of York?"

Clement was aghast. Claude was a legendary archer with a reputation second to none. He was the finest bowman in England and possibly the whole world. He had traveled into Normandy a few years earlier and his father had entertained him. Clement was about eight at the time, and Claude had showed him how to skillfully lay his body into the bow so that he would not be required to use all the strength of his arm.

"Claude of York? He is here?" Clement asked.

"He is here, Clement de la Haye. As is the Rector of Cork, O'Sullivan. Have ye heard of him?"

"Nay. I have not, Tieg. Is he a fair shot?"

"Aye. He might be better than Claude. But then ye will have to get by me as well. I be a better shot than anyone in this town. Can ye beat me Clement de la Haye?"

"He will beat the whole lot of you!" Olaf said excitedly.

Tieg turned his attention to Olaf.

"And who are you by the way? His taller shadow?"

"This is my good and loyal friend, Olaf, son of Halldor," Clement said. "And he is no shadow Tieg."

"Is that so."

"Yes, that is so," Clement replied. "But changing the subject, why does your father want the message from my king that I possess? He is desperate. Why?"

Tieg was smiling. A condescending grin alighted on his round ruddy face.

"If you have a message for Mac Lochlainn like ye say, ye might want to tell me father what it is before he arrives. If not, it may not go well with ye."

"It that a threat, Tieg?"

"Aye, but the threat is not from me or me father. When he warned ye earlier about ye freedom it was not him that ye need fear, but Mac Lochlainn."

Clement thought about this. He did not know what the message from his king to Mac Lochlainn was, as it was sealed with wax and he had given the king his word that it would remain sealed until Mac Lochlainn himself opened it. He had an idea of what it might be though. Was Henry preparing to invade Ireland and looking for an alliance? Or was it a threat? If the latter was the case, then Padraig O'Kane was correct. As the messenger, his life and liberty might be in jeopardy. It is doubtful that Henry knew anything about Mac Lochlainn's character except perhaps that he might be independent and tough to intimidate. By sending a boy in the young Count of la Haye he might have reasoned that Mac Lochlainn would not retaliate against the messenger.

"When is Mac Lochlainn expected to arrive?" Clement asked.

Tieg was chewing on a piece of straw.

"That is why we are giving you this last opportunity to tell us what ye know Clement de la Haye. Our fight is off. Mac Lochlainn is due to arrive at any moment."

"What? I thought that he was to arrive much later in the evening?"

"And so did we. But it is not so, a messenger has warned us," Tieg said with a frown. "He is coming for the games, and we thought he was delayed, but tis not to be. Ye have arrived at the most opportune moment, Clement de la Haye."

Clement thought about what Gorm had told him about Mac Lochlainn. He was in a dangerous situation caught between two warring factions of the Clan U'Neil with his king taking the side of one or the other. This much was now obvious to him. His letter was addressed to Mac Lochlainn as either a warning, or as an expectation that when he invaded Ireland he could count on his support. He decided to take a chance. He would open the letter. Henry had no way of knowing that he would chance upon a rift between Padraig O'Kane and Mac Lochlainn. It was up to him to either diffuse the tension or be the cause of it boiling over.

"Tell your father that I want to talk to him," Clement said suddenly.

Tieg had a cocky smirk on his face knowing that Clement was feeling the pressure.

"I shall return forthright, Clement de la Haye,"

The big Irish boy turned heel and quickly bounded down the staircase. Clement pulled the letter from his cloak. He ran his fingers over the red seal with Henry's crest and for a few seconds he deliberated what to do.

"What are you doing sire?" Olaf asked in a troubled tone.

"I need to find out what this letter says Olaf."

"But...But the seal?"

"I know...I know, but I will think of something."

"Does Mac Lochlainn even know how to read?"

"I do not know Olaf, but I will determine what course of action we need to take after reading this letter."

He carefully pealed the papyrus back breaking the seal and exposing the contents of the letter. It was written in a neat hand in Latin. It was obvious that Henry himself did not write it but dictated the content to his scribe. Clement quickly read it and then read it again. He then folded it neatly and tucked it back into his cloak. His face had lost all color and he felt sick to his stomach.

"What is it? What does it say?" Olaf asked anxiously.

Clement leaned against the parapet wall and looked up at the sky.

"Henry wants Mac Lochlainn to come to England and pay homage to him. He also requires Mac Lochlainn to forfeit his lands in the Ulaid and if he fails to do this, he shall be driven out by force."

Olaf was perplexed.

"But why?"

"I do not know Olaf. I have become involved in some petty squabble, but I am not going to be used like some pawn in a dangerous game of chess!"

As he finished saying this, Tieg appeared once more on the allure, this time followed by his father whose eyes were sparkling. Clement still did not trust him, but from what he had heard about Mac Lochlainn, trusted the Irish high king even less.

"So, you have something to tell me, Clement de la Haye?" Padraig asked condescendingly. "I hope it be worth my effort climbing these steps."

Clement was chewing on his lower lip.

"If I tell you Padraig O'Kane you must first tell me something."

Padraig chuckled lightly.

"What is it that you want to know?"

"There is a rift between you and Mac Lochlainn yet he comes here to break bread with you? Why?"

Padraig's demeanor changed rapidly. His face became serious and he was obviously pondering on whether he needed to tell this youth anything.

"You are wiser than your years, Clement de la Haye, but if you wish to know I will tell you. Mac

Lochlainn is a scoundrel. He invaded the Ulaid and set his will on the people there. The king, my brother, was blinded and taken to the hills where they set him to wander about. He was never seen again. He is testing the waters here. I am not strong enough to oppose him with the few men that are loyal to me. What is the message from your king?"

Clement folded his arms and looked at Padraig and then Tieg who were anxiously waiting for his response. He decided to tell the truth.

"Henry demands that Mac Lochlainn come to England and pay homage. He also requires him to forfeit his lands in the Ulaid or else he shall pay a heavy price."

"An invasion?" Padraig asked incredulously.

"Yes, that is the extent of his message to Mac Lochlainn."

For a few seconds there was an uneasy silence. Then it was interrupted by the sound of horns blaring in the distance. This was followed by the pounding of hooves. Padraig raced to one of the crenels and peered over the edge of the wall.

"It is Mac Lochlainn and he brings a large detachment of his cavalry with him!"

Padraig turned to Clement. A look of desperation on his face.

"You have arrived here for a reason Clement de la Haye," he said, his baggy eyes showing the worry in them.

"I have arrived as a messenger, Padraig O'Kane."

"Then you will tell Mac Lochlainn what you have just told me? I wouldn't want to be you."

Clement stuffed his hands into his cloak and pulled out the letter.

"Or you can tell him on my behalf if you would like," the boy said, handing the parchment to Padraig who whisked it away from him and looked at it. His eyes darting back and forth across the foreign scribbles.

"I cannot read," Padraig said. "You will have to read it to him."

"I have already disobeyed my king by breaking the seal. But I do not like being played, even by kings! King Henry did not trust that I would be brave enough to give Mac Lochlainn a message, hence the secrecy, by sealed letter. I do not fear Mac Lochlainn."

"Then you are a fool!" Padraig exclaimed. "He will have you killed and have your head sent back to Henry in a box as his reply."

Gorm was leaning over the edge of the wall.

"Sire, this vile and wicked man is dangerous. Do not take him lightly. He has at least a hundred men with him."

Clement joined Gorm and Olaf. They had a bird's eye view of the courtyard and stable. There were at least a couple hundred people gathering around. Some were seated on the grassy slopes, while others were milling around in pairs or groups talking. Clement noticed that one of them seemed to be getting a lot of attention. A brooding, vicious looking man with a thick salt and pepper beard. He was wearing a long wool cloak belted at the waist with a huge sword hanging in a scabbard that almost reached the ground. He was giving orders to a few of his men and looking around for something.

"That is Mac Lochlainn sire!" Gorm exclaimed pointing toward the man Clement had noticed.

"He is looking for me. I had better get down there," Padraig said fearfully. He glanced at Clement one last time.

"Remember, I am not your enemy," he said, before departing. Tieg followed him down the stairwell looking back once toward Clement as if he wanted to say something, but dutifully following his father. A few minutes later Clement could see

Padraig and Tieg approaching Mac Lochlainn who was walking in the direction of the pavilion where Dagena and Alice had taken seats with William de Bayeux. Dagena was scanning the crowds that were forming and he knew that she was looking for him. He turned to Gorm.

"Gorm, deliver a message to Jacques for me. Tell him to gather two dozen men on the shore and then merge into the crowds here in the courtyard for the games. Mac Lochlainn will not be aware of what is happening, but I want them ready in case any mischief comes of this."

Gorm was shaking his head.

"Sire, I will do as ye say, but ye must proceed with great caution. This Mac Lochlainn is the devil! I have no doubt he will take your message and try to make an example of ye!"

"I will take my chances Gorm."

A few minutes later Clement and Olaf were mingling in the courtyard and making their way over to the seats under the pavilion where Mac Lochlainn was talking with Padraig and William de Bayeux. William was the first to notice Clement approaching and a mischievous smile broke out on his face.

"Ah! Here he is sire! The one that holds the message from our king," William said loudly so that everyone around them could hear. A dull silence followed as the two boys approached Mac Lochlainn who was seated in a comfortable leather chair raised high on a platform. Olaf stood cautiously off to one side with his hand on the hilt of his sword suspiciously scanning the men around the Irish king. Mac Lochlainn was even more intimidating close up than he was from up above where Clement had got a glance of him. He had a round face with thick black eyebrows. A repulsive red scar ran down his forehead, across his bulbous nose and onto his cheek. He was obviously a man that had seen plenty of combat and was not to be trifled with. He had removed his cloak and set it across his knees exposing his massive bare arms that were loaded with tattoos. He was glaring at Clement with curiosity.

"Ye have a message for me boy? From yer king?"

Clement swallowed hard and wet his lips. He started to speak, but Mac Lochlainn held his hand up.

"Firstly, who are ye?"

"This is the Count de la Haye, your highness," William interrupted.

Mac Lochlainn's head shot around. His grey eyes icy and cold.

"I didn't ask ye!" he screamed in a mixture of Norman and Gaelic. He turned back to Clement.

"I am Clement, Count de la Haye, ambassador to his majesty, King Henry of England," Clement said confidently in Gaelic. He stood in front of the king at the bottom of the platform so that he was forced to look up at him.

"You are a Norman? Or a Dane?"

"I am Norman."

"You are young. King Henry must have faith in you. What is your message?"

Clement reached into his cloak and once again pulled out Henry's letter. Mac Lochlainn's eyes glistened and motioned for him to approach. Clement felt his heart beating rapidly in his chest. As nervous as he was, he tried hard not to let it show. He tried to exude strength and confidence. He glanced at Dagena who had a pensive and worried look on her face. Clement handed the letter to the Irish king who glanced at it and threw it back to him.

"What does it say? Read it!"

Clement read the letter as it was written. He held nothing back. When he was done, he folded it and for some reason stuffed it back into his cloak. Mac Lochlainn was staring at him with a hardened look.

"My king requires an answer," Clement said bravely.

Mac Lochlainn slowly rose to his feet. The silence was deafening as everyone watched, wondering how he was going to respond. He stepped off the platform and towered over the boy who was standing his ground. Dagena had seen enough and she ran in between them and grabbed Clement's arm. Mac Lochlainn was taken aback by the girl's bold move and he broke out into a boisterous laugh.

"Well! I was wondering who this lass might be!"

He took a step back. His hand resting comfortably on the pommel of his sword. Olaf felt his fingers tightening around his hilt.

"You will get my answer...after the games," Mac Lochlainn roared.

He turned to Padraig who was watching the scene with careful interest.

"What are we waiting for! Let the games begin!"

Chapter 8

The herald signaled for the games to begin by blowing through his horn from the turret of the west tower of the castle. A total of fifteen archers gathered in the butts examining their targets to ensure fair play. Each archer was to have an assistant to help handing the shooter arrows and retrieving them from the targets. Clement, of course, chose Olaf. The archers would shoot ten arrows at a target thirty yards away. The top four shooters would then square off in a second round at forty yards and then the top two would compete for champion at the distance of fifty yards. The archers were to shoot by rank. The favorite was to shoot first and the least favorite was to shoot last. Claude of York was by far the favorite archer in the group, followed by O'Sullivan, the Rector of Cork. Tieg, known for his skills was third in the betting odds. Clement, count de la Haye, as an unknown, was dead last. Hundreds of spectators lined the perimeter of the field drinking mead and nibbling on quail and slices of pork. Around the elevated platform where Mac Lochlainn sat, banners and colorful flags flapped in the breeze.

Claude of York leisurely strolled up to the firing line and was handed an arrow by his assistant. He yawned as he let the first one fly. A bullseye dead center in the target. Clement watched him anxiously as he let each one of them fly. After each shot the crowd let out an audible gasp. Ten shots, ten bullseyes. O'Sullivan was next and he performed a similar feat, ten bullseyes. Tieg was next. Unlike the previous two competitors he took his time finding his mark, but each arrow was true. Ten bullseyes. The rest of the shooters had mixed results but each one of them missed the bullseye at least one time. Finally, it was Clement's turn to shoot. When he strode up to the line, he could hear people murmuring and laughing. Although he was the same age as Tieg, he appeared much younger and as an unknown, he was given little respect or chance. Claude of York and O'Sullivan did not even care to watch him shoot and headed for the platform where they engaged in conversation with Mac Lochlainn.

"Give the lad a mug full of goats milk!" came a disrespectful taunt from the crowd.

The audience burst out in laughter. Olaf handed Clement an arrow.

"Do not listen to them sire. Concentrate," Olaf said, encouragingly.

Clement nodded and glanced over at the platform. He could see O'Sullivan attempting to talk to Dagena and Alice, but their attention was wrapped up in what he was about to do. The crowd was inattentive and boisterous. Some people took this time to begin their intermission to prepare for the second round. It was blatant disrespect. They had already brushed off Clement as if he were a non-factor in the game. Only Tieg was attentive. He stood off to the side watching his adversary carefully. Clement loaded the arrow and took aim. Bullseye, dead center. Suddenly the crowd became deathly still. People's heads began to turn back towards the butts, or towards the shooter who calmly loaded his second arrow. The second one lodged right up against the first one. The crowd let out an audible gasp. This got the attention of Claude of York and O'Sullivan who turned to see what all the commotion was about. Clement could see Mac Lochlainn whispering something into Padraig O'Kane's ear. The third arrow landed in the bullseye but to the upper left of the first two arrows. The fourth one in the bullseye to the upper right. The final six arrows formed a semi-circle in the bullseye below the first two. It was Claude of York who first noticed what Clement had done. He turned to Mac Lochlainn who had stood up and casually stepped off the platform onto the shooting field to get a better look at the target. Clement had created a smiley face with the arrows. His unbelievable accomplishment began to spread through the crowd who began cheering with cries of astonishment.

Clement and Olaf approached the target where they met Claude, Padraig and Mac Lochlainn who were admiring the placement of the arrows with something bordering the incredible.

"Who are you lad?" Claude asked, his wrinkled brow twitching. "Where did you learn to shoot like this?"

"He is Clement, count de la Haye," Dagena answered for him. She had boldly stridden into the circle of admirers and threw her arm around his shoulder. "And no one can shoot like him. Except maybe me!"

Clement's face was beaming proudly as his eyes met hers.

"You do not remember me Claude of York, but I remember you," Clement said. "You once showed me the proper way of handling a bow."

"Aye, I remember now Clement de la Haye. It appears that I showed you too well, lad!" he exclaimed with a chuckle.

Claude held out his hand and Clement took it. Mac Lochlainn pulled one of the arrows from the target and was examining it carefully. He handed it to Claude who merely glanced at it.

"Can you outshoot this boy?"

"Nay. I concede. I am good, but not that good. It is pointless to continue."

Mac Lochlainn then turned to O'Sullivan who gave him the same answer. He then turned to Tieg who was standing aloof with his father.

"Tieg O'Kane! What about you? Can you do this?"

Tieg did not respond for a moment, as if he were pondering the possibility of continuing, and then without uttering a word shook his head. A jealous expression crossing his face as he peered at Clement.

"Then it is settled. Clement de la Haye is champion." Mac Lochlainn said, reluctantly eying the boy with a look of hate. "Let us continue to the next event."

There was a short intermission during which the butts were cleared of the targets and straw was laid down in an oval patch in the center of the courtyard. It was now dark and torches had been set up to lighten the field so that people could get a good view of the contestants who were to do battle. Clement noticed that Mac Lochlainn was conversing with Padraig O'Kane. They seemed to be in disagreement about something, but he was too far away to ascertain what it was that they were talking about.

Since he had won the archery competition, Clement had become a celebrity of sorts. People that had been jeering him earlier were now praising his youth and ability and wondering who this upstart archer was. While the groundskeepers were preparing the wrestling arena, he retired into one of the smaller gardens with Olaf, Dagena and Alice. He noticed William of Bayeux lurking in the shadows talking with Tieg and another man whom he did not recognize.

"I don't like it sire," Olaf said. "There is some mischief afoot."

Clement was cracking his knuckles and looking like he was ready for a fight.

"I am with Olaf, Clement," Dagena said. "While you were shooting, I overheard Mac Lochlainn telling Padraig O'Kane to secure the castle for the night. What would he mean by that comment except to keep us prisoners? You have delivered the king's message. Can we not slip out of here back to the ships?"

Clement shook his head.

"Impossible Dagena. At the moment, there are only a handful of our men on shore. There is no way that we could leave unseen."

"Well, what are we going to do?" she asked nervously.

"We bide our time. Padraig despises Mac Lochlainn. He thinks of him as a usurper. Mac Lochlainn has underestimated me."

Dagena was about to respond when they noticed Tieg approaching them.

"That was some fine shooting Clement de la Haye. Are you ready to try your hand at wrestling?"

Clement had a scowl on his face.

"I do believe that Olaf is fighting in my steed good sir, but if you would rather take me on. I will be happy to oblige you."

Tieg chuckled.

"It is not my decision. Have you not heard? Mac Lochlainn wants to see the famous archer try his hand against the son of Padraig."

Tieg clapped Clement on the back and confidently strolled away.

"He is twice your size Clement. You won't stand a chance!" Olaf exclaimed.

"And you would stand a better chance Olaf? I am not afraid of Teig O'Kane. It is a wrestling match, not a fight to the death."

Suddenly there was a blast from the trumpet followed by the beating of a drum. When they returned to the courtyard two brawny men stripped to the waist were squaring off against one another on the straw. The crowd let out a barbaric yawl when one of the contestants grabbed the other in a strong headlock and began to beat him with his fist.

Dagena grabbed Clement's arm and pointed to the two combatants.

"Is that what you call a wrestling match Clement? They are beating each other to death!"

Clement swallowed hard.

"Aye, it appears that these Irish have a different way of exercising their strength than us Normans."

"I told you sire," Olaf said. "They are savages! I am taking your place. If I call out Tieg, he will have to face me or they will think him a coward."

Olaf started to remove his cloak, but Clement stopped him.

"And what shall they think of me if you take my place Olaf? Nay, I shall face him."

Dagena stepped in between the two boys with a scowl on her face.

"Enough! There is no honor or chivalry in this! No one is facing him. We are getting out of here."

Before she could say anything else the match had ended with one of the men unconscious and being carried out of the circle. Mac Lochlainn stood up and pointed at Tieg.

"Tieg O'Kane! You will fight the champion of archers, Clement de la Haye!"

Mac Lochlainn was standing on the elevated platform with his hands on his hips. He was wearing a broad smile and the red scar on his face seemed to be even more hideous highlighted by the torch light. Padraig O'Kane appeared nervous. He approached Mac Lochlainn to say something but the Irish king brushed him aside.

"No rules! You fight until one fighter is rendered senseless!"

The crowd broke into cheers and pandemonium erupted. People began throwing things into the circle where Tieg had already stripped himself to the waist and was waiting for his opponent who stood glaring at him from the sidelines.

"No Clement. You can't do this!" Dagena screamed. "He will kill you!"

Clement ignored her. He had already removed his hat and cloak and handed it to Olaf and was in the process of taking off his boots when she grabbed him by the arm.

"I won't let this happen!"

"It is too late to stop it," Clement said softly. "Do not worry about me Dagena. I always find a way...do I not?"

She turned to Olaf who had a grave look on his face.

"Do something Olaf!" she screamed.

"I will not let my lord be killed," he said. "Do not fear Dagena. If the contest gets out of hand, I will stop it!"

Dagena started to follow Clement out into the field of battle, but Alice stepped in her way.

"Let it go Dagena. Have faith in Clement. He will find a way. He always does."

She led her friend back to the perimeter of the field. Clement slowly approached Tieg who was circling back and forth at the far end of the circle nearest the platform. The bigger boy began shadow boxing and in the few seconds that Clement was able to watch he noticed a few flaws in his arsenal that he might be able to take advantage of. Mac Lochlainn gave the signal and the herald blew the horn. For a minute or so both boys circled each other. Tieg knew that he was stronger than his opponent, but after seeing what Clement could do on the archery field, he wisely proceeded with caution.

"How will we settle this Tieg O'Kane?" Clement asked, as they circled one another looking for an opportunity.

Tieg responded with a devious smile. Instead of answering his opponent with words he went for a takedown, but Clement leaped out of his way avoiding the first aggressive action of the fight. The crowd booed. They wanted to see blood. Tieg attacked again, this time managing to grab Clement's left leg and taking him off his feet. Clement landed hard on his back but when Tieg attempted to follow up by pouncing on him, the smaller boy easily rolled away causing Tieg to land hard on his shoulder in the sawdust. Clement was back on his feet and soon the two boys were circling each other again. This time Clement went on the offensive. He lashed out with his fists. A left hook connected with Tieg's chin, and Clement followed this with a right which smashed into his jaw rattling the bigger boy who tasted blood for the first time. The crowd began chanting Tieg's name, but some of them were siding with the stranger who against all odds was holding his own against a boy who had never been bested in a competitive match before. Tieg wiped the blood away from his mouth and quickly peered up at the platform where Mac Lochlainn stood frowning.

It was now Tieg's turn to go on the offensive. He began to swing his fists wildly but Clement was able to block each one of them except for the last one which landed on his jaw knocking him to the ground. For a few seconds, Clement saw stars and could taste the sweetness of his own blood from a cut on his lip. He stood up just in time to see Tieg barreling toward him, but the bigger boy misjudged his opponents condition and went for a flying tackle which Clement avoided by adroitly stepping out of the way. Clement countered by jumping on Tieg's back and grabbing him around the neck. Tieg lost his balance and ended up falling backwards with Clement still attached to him pulling back on his neck. Tieg, however, was now able to play his weight to his advantage and slowly turned himself around so that Clement no longer had the upper hand. Pinned beneath the bigger boy Clement attempted to keep his lock on Tieg's neck but eventually the son of Padraig was able to slip out of it. Now Clement found himself in real trouble. Tieg began to rain down punches which Clement did his best to block.

Dagena began to scream and Olaf was just about to intervene when Clement found a burst of adrenaline and to Tieg's surprise, managed to catch one of his punches and using both hands turned Tieg's arm so that the bigger boy was forced to adjust his position. This was all Clement needed to roll away and he was quickly on his feet again. There was a trickle of blood running down his nose, and he could feel his left eye starting to swell, but he was not beaten yet. Once again Tieg came on. Clement sidestepped him and caught the bigger boy with a right hook against his right eye that stunned Tieg and almost knocked him down. Tieg now realized that Clement, as small as he was, was no pushover. He could fight. Both boys now circled each other looking for a weakness. Tieg attacked again this time grabbing Clement around the waist and bringing him down to the ground hard and knocking the wind out of him. Straddling the smaller boy, he raised his fist to strike him but noticed that Clement's eyes had become glassy. He was almost unconscious and Tieg realized that if he hit him again, he might kill him. With his fist still raised he heard a commanding voice behind him.

"Finish him! Kill him!"

Tieg glanced behind him and could see that Mac Lochlainn had entered the field of battle and was standing with his hands resting on his hips. An imperious look of hate on his face.

"I said kill him! That is my message to King Henry!"

Dagena and Olaf started to run out to help Clement but were immediately surrounded by a half a dozen of Mac Lochlainn's men.

For a few seconds Tieg remained where he was, his fist still raised for the kill. Blood trickled from his nose, and his right eye was swelling shut. He had been in a battle. He glanced down at Clement who was starting to regain his senses, but instead of striking the fatal blow, he stood up and offered his valiant opponent his hand. Clement reached up and took it and Tieg hauled him to his feet. Clement was standing on wobbly legs and Tieg grabbed his arm and threw it around his shoulder to help him stand.

"If you don't kill him, I will kill you both!" Mac Lochlainn screamed angrily.

Tieg was grinding his teeth but said nothing. Padraig O'Kane approached the scene timidly. His hand on the hilt of his sword. Mac Lochlainn turned toward him.

"Stay where you are Padraig O'Kane. I am your king and sovereign lord!"

"Sire...I..."

"Shut your mouth coward!"

Mac Lochlainn began to advance toward the two boys. He had drawn his sword from his scabbard. His face glowing menacingly in the torchlight. The silence was deafening as people watched to see what was about to transpire. Tieg began to move backwards taking Clement with him.

"I ask you again Tieg O'Kane!"

Tieg pointed at Mac Lochlainn, the blood running from his nose down onto his chest. His swollen lips were quivering slightly. Clement had done a job on him.

"You are no king who will order me to do such a thing!" Tieg screamed. "I'll not kill this boy who has fought bravely and with great honor. If thou wish to kill him you will have to kill me first!"

Mac Lochlainn's eyes glowed with hate and there was rage and death in them. Clement glanced behind them and could see Olaf slipping away from the men who had restrained him, as they were now preoccupied with what their leader was doing. Mac Lochlainn suddenly lunged forward with his sword. Tieg reacted swiftly by pushing Clement away from the blade's arc which caught the son of Padraig with a glancing blow across his left shoulder. Tieg let out a painful scream and fell into the sawdust. Clement had fallen to the ground and the next thing that he knew he could see Olaf charging toward him and he knew what his friend's intentions were. Olaf had his dagger out but was too far from Mac Lochlainn to use it. Clement gave him the signal that he was ready and Olaf threw the dagger at Clement's feet. It landed with the ivory handle up, the tempered blade sticking into the sawdust. Clement felt dizzy and the rest of what happened he barely remembered. With wobbly legs and hazy vision, he retrieved the dagger and staggered to his feet. He turned to see Mac Lochlainn with his sword raised getting ready to strike the life out of Tieg O'Kane. With careful aim he let the dagger fly. It entered Mac Lochlainn's back and the Irish king became immobile almost immediately. He dropped his sword and reached around him in confusion. He could see the young Count of la Haye who had dropped to his knees. Clement felt the whole world spinning and the last thing he remembered before passing out and falling flat on his face was the benevolent form of Dagena rushing toward him.

Chapter 9

Clement slept for nearly twelve hours. He had been taken to Tieg's room where the son of Padraig had also been taken. Both boys, former combatants now sharing the large, feathered bed where they were being attended to by Dagena and Alice. Jacques sat in a chair outside of the room with orders from Dagena to allow no one entry. No exceptions.

Olaf had taken charge of Dunseverick Castle after Clement had collapsed on the field of battle. Unknown to the unconscious young count, his foresight had paid off. Jacques and the men he had brought with him immediately set to work disarming Mac Lochlainn's men. They were then expelled from the castle's grounds and had their horses confiscated.

Clement awoke in a hazy daze. The first thing he recognized was what he thought was an angel hovering over him. He reached up towards it and felt a hand grasp his fingers. It was a tender hand and awareness and clarity finally came to him. It was not an angel at all, but Dagena. She kissed his hand and he smiled.

"Dagena, how...how long have I been sleeping?"

"Nearly twelve hours Clement. The sun has risen again, but you need to rest. Try not to talk."

"Mac Lochlainn?"

"Dead. You killed him."

"And Tieg O'Kane?"

He heard someone chuckle.

"Well...I could be better. No thanks to you, Clement de la Haye," Tieg said jokingly. "Let me see. I have a swollen eye, a broken nose, fractured rib and a bloody lip."

Clement attempted to raise himself up on his elbow, but painfully realized that he too had a fractured rib, and one of his eyes was shut. His arms were also bruised where he had attempted to defend himself from Tieg's blows.

"For a little fellow ye sure do pack a powerful punch Clement de la Haye."

Clement sighed. "Aye, as do you Tieg O'Kane,"

"Ye saved my life Clement de la Haye. I will not soon forget that."

"And you saved mine Tieg O'Kane. I will not soon forget that."

Alice appeared at Tieg's side with a bowl of water, some fresh linen and some herbs.

"Time to change your shoulder bandage Tieg," she said calmly.

Tieg winced, remembering how bad it had stung when Alice first cleaned it. "Aye, that time again, is it? Well, that wound will be the last one that Mac Lochlainn will ever inflict on anyone thanks to Clement."

"He sliced you with his blade?" Clement asked.

Tieg grimaced as Alice peeled the linen away from his wound. She had made a plaster with herbs from the garden.

"Aye, Clement, when I pushed ye away he came down with the blade. If I had not been quicker, I'd not be sitting here talking to ye."

Clement could still taste blood in his mouth from his swollen lip and looked at his hands which were bandaged from using them on Tieg's head. Tieg noticed him examining them.

"Aye, I have a thick skull Clement de la Haye. Sorry about that."

Both boys began to laugh and Clement reached over with his left hand and Tieg grasped it in friendship.

"Why do boys have to fight?" Dagena asked, placing a wet cloth on Clement's swollen eye. "It is so barbaric. Look at the both of you? You look like a couple of heathens all busted up like this. And now you sit here and reminisce about it! Alice and I should go out and let you fend for yourselves."

"Well, Mac Lochlainn is the one that made us fight like that Dagena," Clement said. "One day I will have to show Tieg O'Kane how we do it in Normandy. By the way, where has Olaf run off to?"

"He is supervising the trading of goods with my father," Tieg said.

Clement sat up, letting the wet cloth fall from his eye. "Is he now? Well, I have slept enough. Tis time for me to rise and see the morning."

"Oh no you're not!" Dagena exclaimed imperiously. "You are staying right here Clement. You can thank Tieg O'Kane for that and Tieg O'Kane can thank Clement de la Haye for being in the same situation!"

She gently pushed him back down on the bed and he looked over at Tieg who was smirking.

"Aye, Clement. I have already tried it before you woke up. Ye best listen to the lady!"

They both broke out in laughter. Then Clement became serious.

"Well, we have eliminated a blight from this land and King Henry will be pleased."

"Aye," Tieg said. "And ye can count on the O'Kane's being staunch allies."

"Who taught you the tongue of the Norman's Tieg," Dagena asked, placing the wet linen back on Clement's eye.

"My father, yet he cannot read that well. Though I can. Not all of us Irish fester in ignorance. I also speak some Latin, but we have very few books here. I wish that we had more, but I only have a Latin bible and Father Fergus gave me a copy of Herodotus' Histories.

Clement became excited.

"You have a tome of Herodotus' Histories?"

"Aye, do you read too Clement?"

"Indeed! I have read Herodotus. I have brought along a handful of books with me on the voyage, Tieg. Caesar's History of Gaul and Monmouth's History, among others.

"Can I see them?"

"Certainly. I shall have someone fetch them from the ship."

Dagena was sitting by the bed with her arms folded. She was shaking her head.

"Well, together you have two good eyes out of the four so maybe you both can read something between them!" she said with wry amusement.

The two boys looked at each other and noticed each other's swollen black eyes and burst out laughing at the same time.

The days passed quickly and soon it was time for the fleet to once again take to the seas. It had been almost a week since Clement's encounter with Mac Lochlainn and, in that time, he had shored up his alliance with the O'Kane's. In one stroke he had eliminated a threat to King Henry in Ireland. What Henry decided to do from this point on rested with him. Clement de la Haye had done his part and more. It was now time to move on.

Before departing, Clement had given his copy of Monmouth to Tieg O'Kane as a gift and

Tieg, in return, gave Clement his copy of Herodotus. From the Green Ship, Clement and Dagena watched the majestic cliffs of Ireland recede in the distance. As they were rounding the coast, they passed by a landmark that none of them would ever forget. Thousands of strange looking basaltic rocks that rose in tall columns stretched out into the sea.

"I have never seen anything like it," Dagena commented.

Gorm was wearing a broad smile on his face.

"Aye, tis a causeway made by a giant named Fin Macool at some remote time in the past. I have stood on those rocks many years ago and I can tell ye that there is something magical about the place."

"Well, I would not mind exploring the place, but twill have to wait until our return." Clement said, using his glass to get a better look. He then handed it to Dagena. It was near dusk and the rays of the setting sun reflected off the rocks giving it a reddish-orange brilliance that seemed to heighten its surreal appearance.

It was soon dark and the fleet of ships left the Irish coast behind them. It was a calm night and when morning came there was no land in sight in any direction. Clement took a reading with the astrolabe and recorded it in his log. They were headed northwest where he hoped to find the coast of the Norse settlers.

"I want a man in the crow's nest at all times," Clement told Pierre, who set up a watch. He stood on top of the sterncastle with Adam who followed Clement around the ship like a tall shadow. A few of the archers, including Esteban also joined him, each choosing a crenel to lean on as they looked out across the wide expanse of ocean. The horizon seemed hazy, limitless and foreboding. Clement could see the rest of his fleet trailing behind in his wake. William of Bayeux, as usual, was trailing well behind the others in the Brown Ship.

"Clement want to play knucklebones with Adam? Clement play knucklebones with Adam?"

Clement turned toward his giant friend and smiled.

"We just played knucklebones Adam."

"I'll play a game with you Adam," Osment said from the top of the rope ladder. "Go below and I will meet you at the table. Just give me a minute with Clement."

"Oh! Oh! Yes! Adam play knucklebones with Osment!"

Adam hurried down the ladder and landed with a jumping thud on the deck. Osment reached into his cloak and pulled out his ledger and opened it.

"Before we left the Irish coast, Ceres and Sir Roger gave me a complete inventory of their vessels, but I was met with derision by Sir William. He told me that it was none of my business and that he would handle the inventory of his own vessel."

Clement pursed his lips together in anger and slammed his fist into the palm of his hand.

"That man is intolerable, Osment!"

Osment cringed.

"I'm sorry Clement. I know you wanted it, but Sir William insisted that I leave his presence. As he is second in command of the fleet, I could not insist otherwise."

Clement looked out across the sea toward the Brown Ship.

"It's not your fault Osment. I will handle him when I next see him face to face. So, what are your calculations?"

Osment pointed to a column in the ledger that listed 'item' and then ran his finger across the page.

"I have broken it up into types of victuals and non-perishables. I have also calculated how long the food will last by rationing. For a six-month voyage without restocking, we are in good condition at the current rate of consumption. However, we must anticipate spoilage and the possibility of not being able to replenish our stock."

Clement examined the numbers and notes that Osment had made in the far column. "You have done well Osment. I thank thee. We will cast the nets in a few days to see if we can gather some fresh fish to supplement our stock."

"Aye, Clement. That will be good. One more thing. We have plenty of chicory root. I recommend that we brew enough of it to give a daily dose to the crew. A few men are complaining of the gum sickness."

Clement was puzzled. "The gum sickness?"

"Aye, the tongue gets patchy and swells. The gums bleed and then the teeth start to fall out. Some call it the scurvy. It can be fatal."

"How do you know of this?" Clement asked.

Osment pointed to his skull. "I have been studying the anatomy of the human body. It is a strange vessel that can adapt to many changes, but one thing is certain. It requires certain foods to function properly. I do not know why, but if a person lacks fruits or vegetables the body will start to deteriorate. It will exhibit certain symptoms that will eventually worsen if not treated."

Clement was rubbing his chin in deep thought as he perused the columns in Osment's ledger. "And you believe that the chicory root can cure this illness?"

"Indeed, I do."

"Then I leave it up to you to implement the remedy as you see fit. I thank thee Osment."

Osment pointed to the Brown Ship in the distance. "And what about them and the other ships? We should tell them so that they can implement this same remedy."

"None of those vessels are equipped with a way to brew chicory water. They will have to digest the leaves in other ways. But they shall be warned of this danger."

Esteban was listening to the conversation and joined the two boys who had digressed into another topic. Clement's master of archers was a big lad of sixteen. Besides Clement himself, no one on the ship could match his skill with the bow. He had been a playmate of the young count for as long as either of them could remember, as his mother had been a servant at the castle. She had died when Esteban was ten and Count Hugo had let the boy train as a knight, first serving as a page in his service. His archery skills were immediately recognized, and Clement had promoted him as his Captain of archers. Clement had offered him a sleeping berth in one of the castles, but Esteban preferred sleeping out under the stars on the deck unless the weather was bad.

"Sire, I might suggest that we let the men set up the butts and get their practice in. They are a little restless. Perhaps we can have a competitive match," Esteban said, chewing on a sliver of wood.

Clement nodded. "That is a splendid idea Esteban, however, they might find it rather rough finding the bullseye with the continuous rolling of the ship, eh?"

"Perhaps, we will see. I will set something up tomorrow."

"Archery practice on the high seas...I never would have thought of it," Clement said with a smile.

The rest of the day was quiet. That evening, before dark, Clement decided to open the sealed letter from King Henry but wanted to do so alone. He knew that the king had told him to wait until he was 100 leagues from the Irish coast. He knew that he was less than that but he concluded that it did not matter. He had already disobeyed one of Henry's orders, so why not make it two? Anyway, only he would know and he was curious to find out the substance of the letter. He ordered everyone out of the sterncastle including Dagena who had grabbed the letter from the table and jokingly made Clement chase her around it before giving it back to him. When he was all alone, he sat next to the small fire pit and using the dim light, he broke the wax seal. Before unfolding the document, he felt strangely uneasy. Why was he nervous? What could the document possibly contain to cause him to feel this way? Almost certainly it had something to do with further instructions. His eyes focused and he began to read.

Clement de la Haye,

You are now a hundred leagues west of the Hibernian coast. Your orders:

1. *Once you arrive at this place called Vinland ascertain the whereabouts of Sir Humphrey Rochford's fleet.*

2. *The vessels are laden with treasure. There is a gold chest, secured with silver bands and a bronze seal with the image of two knights on horseback. I want you to retrieve this chest and bring it back to me at Chinon Castle. Do not open the chest. It is imperative that the chest remains sealed.*

3. *I do believe that Sir William de Bayeux is a spy in the service of King Louis. He does not know that I know and you will not tell him that you know. Make use of his services and this information as you see fit.*

4. *Destroy this correspondence. It is for your eyes only to behold.*

Henry Rex

Clement read the letter a second time. He sighed and began to rub his chin. He was in deep thought. What manner of business had he gotten himself into? He held the letter up against the flames and read it a third time. He knew immediately that he was going to disobey one of Henry's orders. He might destroy the letter, but he had already decided that he would confide with Dagena and Olaf. He thought about telling Pierre or Jacques, and maybe Osment and Alice, but the less people that knew, the better. Dagena and Olaf were his closest confidants. If Wedem were here he would tell him, but Wedem was many miles away. He stood up and went to the door and peered out into the dusk. He could see Dagena leaning on the bulwark talking to Trousett who noticed Clement first.

"Sire is there something I can do to help you?" the cartographer asked intrusively.

Clement decided that he liked Trousett, but this was not meant for his ears. He was a loyal servant of Henry and was almost certainly along on the voyage to act as eyes and ears for the king.

"I need to talk to Dagena,"

Dagena shuffled over to him. She could see the concern on his face.

"Get Olaf," he whispered. "I need to speak with both of you in private. Try not to raise suspicion. I don't want any prying ears."

"What's wrong?" she murmured.

"I'll tell you both at the same time."

She hurried off and Clement slipped back into the sterncastle. He quickly sat down next to the fire and held the letter up again to read it. He could hear the wind whipping across the deck outside and although the sea was calm, he could not help but think that there might be a storm brewing somewhere in the distance. Before he had left, he had been working on an experiment where he might be able to predict the weather with a device that could measure pressure. He had stored the material in one of his crates, but he had not had the time to work on it. Perhaps now would be a good time to test it, but first he needed his friend's advice.

The door opened and Dagena and Olaf entered.

"Shut the door," Clement said. "I just opened King Henry's letter."

Dagena folded her arms, her mouth curled into a sarcastic smile. She sat down next to Clement who was still holding the letter possessively, as if its contents might spill out onto the floor and begin speaking to others.

"Uh...we know Clement. That is why we left you to have a private moment. Are you going to share the contents of the letter, or do we have to guess?"

He pursed his lips together and nodded, handing Dagena the letter. Olaf slid down next to her and together they read it.

"Sir William is a spy!" Dagena declared loudly.

Clement cringed. "Lower your voice Dagena," he whispered angrily. "Do you want the whole crew to know?"

"Sorry Clement, but this is serious. What are we going to do?"

Olaf stood up and shoved his thumbs into the seams of his doublet.

"Well, what we are not going to do Dagena, is tell anyone else about the contents of this letter."

Clement clasped his hands behind his head and leaned back, closing his eyes.

"Correct Olaf, we tell no one. And Sir William is the least of my worries. I do believe that I am being played by King Henry and I do not like it. I was told to find out the reason for Sir Humphrey's mission and was understood that this was to be a voyage of exploration. It now appears to have become one of strategic importance and I am now tasked with destroying Sir Humphrey's fleet!"

Olaf looked perplexed. "It doesn't say anything about that in the letter sire."

Clement sighed. "Well how does he expect me to acquire that chest? Does he think that if I ask nicely, Sir Humphrey will just hand it over?"

"No, you are right Clement," Dagena said, sprinkling some chicory leaves in the pot and placing it on the hook over the fire. "The letter does not state it boldly, but it is implied."

"Well, I wonder what the devil is in that chest?" Olaf asked seriously. "It must be something of great importance or he would not have trusted you with this mission. And why did he let Sir William take charge of one of the ships when he knew for a fact that he was a spy? This makes no sense."

Clement was watching Dagena use a ladle to stir the chicory water.

"Well, it might be a moot point anyway. The chance of us finding Sir Humphrey's fleet is extremely low. We may not even be able to locate this place known as Vinland, though if anyone can find it, I can. I do believe that I know the general location by direction, but exactly how far, I cannot say. Another thing that puzzles me is this Sir Humphrey Rochford. No one seems to know who he is. King Henry does not even know him. I have never heard of him, nor has anyone else. Who is he? And where does he come from? How is it that he is entrusted with a voyage of this magnitude by one of the most powerful kings in all of Christendom? I must say that I am completely baffled by the whole business, but I intend on finding out."

Dagena pulled the ladle out of the water and tasted it. She winked at the two boys and filled their mugs. Clement took a sip and forced a smile. He peered through a knothole in the bulkhead and could see the sky, stark and gray behind them. Somewhere back there, was the coast of Ireland, with its green pastures and rolling hills and dales. Beyond that, England and Normandy, where his castle sat, now a distant memory. He stretched and almost spilled his chicory water. He sat down cross legged in front of the fire and placed his mug down in front of him. The steam lifting from it in wavy swirls.

"Do not worry Clement," Dagena said soothingly. "We are in this together. We will figure it out."

Clement held his hands up to the fire, feeling its warmth. "Well, I wish that I had more foresight. I do not appreciate being played with."

"Henry doesn't know who he is playing with," Olaf said. "He is using you for your skills in navigation and cartography. You also happen to have in your possession the greatest vessel in Normandy. He thinks your youth will keep you under his spell. An obsequious vassal, afraid to strike out on his own. He believes that you will bend to his iron will, but he has underestimated you sire! Also, you have us to help you...right Dagena!"

Dagena raised her mug in salute. "Like I said, we are in this together."

Clement and Olaf lifted their mugs and clinked them together with Dagena's in a toast. Olaf's mug tipped a little too much and some of the hot fluid spilled onto the deck causing Clement and Dagena to laugh.

"I never did trust Sir William," Olaf said. "He is a like an asp ready to strike. I am going to watch him like a hawk, Clement."

"Aye," Clement said, "but we must be cautious of King Henry's warning. There is a reason he let Sir William take command of one of the vessels. We need to find out why. Something tells me that Sir William knows what is in that chest and Henry knows it."

"But why keep it a secret from you?" Dagena asked.

"I do not know but I intend to find out."

Dagena thought about this and then held a finger up. With her free hand she was brushing the strands of red hair out of her eyes.

"What if Sir William is not a spy at all? What if King Henry is using you to get him to this place, Vinland and then he will usurp your command, seize your ship and have you imprisoned or killed. After all, did he not want to place his men on the Green Ship? Perhaps by telling you that he is a spy he thinks that you will try to have him arrested and this might give him the excuse to take command."

Clement thought about this and had to admit that she made a good point.

"Dagena might be right Clement." Olaf said worriedly. "We have only about 25 men loyal to you on this one ship while he has over 100 on the other three ships. We will have to be careful."

Clement buried his blond head in his hands and when he looked up, he was smiling. "This is the reason why I have confided in the two of you."

He glanced at the letter again and then crinkling it up in his hands, he pitched it into the flames watching them lick it up. He could hear the creaking of the deck and flapping of the sail outside, crisp and steady as the wind carried them further into the unknown.

Chapter 10

It was a calm, frigid afternoon about a week after Clement had opened King Henry's letter, when the lookout in the crow's nest spotted a small dark mass on the surface of the water off to the north-west. Almost immediately, the starboard side of the vessel was crowded with Jacques' men-at-arms and Esteban's archers who strained their eyes to catch a glimpse of the object, but being much lower than the man above, they could see nothing but the gray and hazy distance. The dark water lapping and foaming along the side of the ship was the only noise they could hear as each person dwelled in their own silence, watching and waiting. Finally, another shout confirmed it. Pierre had spotted the object from the top of the sterncastle.

Clement darted into the cabin to grab his glass. Swift as a cat he flew up the ladder followed closely by Dagena. Olaf and Alice were already there. Pierre pointed to the spot. He was wagging his finger with excitement.

"There sire! Point your glass there! Tis a flat iceberg maybe?"

The young count held the glass up to his left eye and peered through the magnified lens. At first, he could see nothing, but then it came into focus. Whatever it was, it was gigantic. He swallowed hard and attempted to focus again.

"It is moving!" he yelled into the frigid air.

The sea, he knew at this latitude, was dotted with large icebergs. Some of them as tall as cathedrals, glistening white and blue, like mighty fortresses that guarded the sea. This was no iceberg. Whatever it was, it was clearly alive or being controlled by something that was living. He turned to Pierre.

"Have all men on deck under arms at once!"

"Yes sire."

Pierre scurried down the ladder and disappeared. They could hear him barking orders below and the sound of men running across the deck.

Clement leaned over the railing that overlooked the deck. "Esteban, help Gorm up here as quick as possible. He needs to see this."

"As you wish sire," the captain of archers replied.

Esteban attempted to assist Gorm, but the old man brushed him off.

"Nay young fellow. I may be an old sea dog but I need no assistance in climbing the ladder.

When I do, ye can have a board ready and can help cast me body into the sea!"

"But my Lord Clement insists that I help thee," Esteban pleaded.

"My Lord Clement means well but old Gorm can manage."

Clement had given the glass to Dagena who was being harassed by Olaf to take his turn looking through it.

"It is moving quite rapidly just beneath the surface of the water! Look at the ripple!" Dagena exclaimed excitedly.

Gorm's old arthritic fingers reached the top rung of the ladder and he adroitly, for his advanced age, reached the top of the sterncastle. Clement had glanced around in time to see him pulling himself up using the rails as support. The boy count rushed over and grabbed the old man's arm to support him.

"Esteban!" Clement yelled angrily.

"He wouldn't let me help him my lord!"

Gorm was half grinning and half attempting to regain his breath. His ruddy, sun scorched nose twitching.

"Gorm, you could have fallen and broken your neck!" Clement said sternly.

"Aye sire, but I didn't."

"Dagena, give Gorm the glass."

She was about to hand it to Olaf, but turned to the old man instead, who had stumbled over to the crenel and peered over the edge. Gorm held the glass up to his aged eye and the grin immediately left his face. It was replaced by an expression of doubt, mixed with wonder.

"What is it?" Dagena asked anxiously.

Gorm ignored her, holding the glass steady and whistling softly to himself. Finally, he lowered it and handed it back to her. Olaf immediately snatched it.

Dagena was impatient. "Well? Do you have any idea?"

"Aye, my lady. I have heard of this leviathan but have never actually seen one until now. I do believe I mentioned it to you and my Lord Clement after we encountered that great sea serpent on the way to the Island of Fire, two seasons ago. Tis called a kraken. We will have to be careful, perhaps steer to the south and avoid antagonizing this dreaded beast."

Once more Clement rushed over to the ladder.

"Pierre, furl the sail and have some of the men man the oars and row south!"

"What about the other ships?"

"Send them the signal."

"Aye, it shall be done sire," Pierre responded.

Olaf was now looking through the glass.

"It has disappeared beneath the surface! I can no longer see it!"

Baldwin appeared on the deck with Bran and blew through the trumpet, giving due warning of the impending danger. Clement hoped that they would hear it and were being vigilant. He could see Ceres in the Red Ship off the port bow while Sir Roger in the Black Ship was trailing in its wake. Sir William, in the Brown Ship was almost invisible in the haze, lagging somewhat behind, as usual, on the starboard side.

Olaf was still glancing through the glass with Alice clinging to his arm wanting to take a turn looking through it.

"There it is again!" Olaf screamed. "It is off the port bow!"

By now most everyone could see the massive lump of scaly flesh appearing as a dark mass in the distance. It was irregular and seemed to have no form, most of its body submerged in the cold dark depths. Clement felt a knot in his stomach. The leviathan was still a great distance from the ship, and he wondered if it had even seen them. Perhaps it was just passing by them on its way to wherever its destination might be. He did not know, but he had to be prepared for all possibilities. He was about to take another look through the glass when he heard a commotion down below.

Osment came bounding up the ladder followed by Adam who had sort of become the red-haired boy's assistant. In fact, the gentle giant now spent more time following Osment around than he did Clement.

"Clement, there is another one of those things below the ship!"

Clement's eyes widened.

"What? How do you know?"

"A few of us caught a glimpse of it as it passed beneath us. It is at least the length of the ship, perhaps more!"

"Where is it now?"

Osment pointed toward the port side of the vessel.

"It disappeared in that direction."

The other monster had also vanished. Olaf was hunting for it with the glass, but the sea remained calm. Gorm strolled over to one of the crenels on the port side, his face haggard and lined, but his demeanor cool.

"It is rare to see one of these creatures," he said calmly, "never mind two of them! They rarely surface, or so I have been told by those that have seen them."

He turned to address Clement, but the boy count was gone. He had descended the ladder in two quick, agile jumps and was on the main deck and into the sterncastle in a few seconds. He hurried over to his supply chest under his bunk where he kept all his nautical instruments. Typically, he kept this locked with a spring lock and he reached into his cloak for the key. He was so nervous that he almost dropped it. Fumbling with it, he managed to insert it into the lock with his cold fingers and then opened the lid. He began removing his instruments and tools and when he had everything out, he removed the false bottom and glanced into the secret compartment. He felt a presence hovering over his shoulder and turned quickly.

"Dagena?"

She wore a puzzled look. The wool cap on her head askew, with her long red locks hanging around it as if they issued forth from it instead of her scalp.

"You surprised me."

"Why so secretive Clement? Are you hiding something from me?"

The boy smiled, showing his teeth.

"Do you remember when the Green Ship was attacked by those pirates that were holding Olaf captive?"

She wrinkled her brow and began stroking her chin.

"Yes, of course I do...why?"

"Well, I made an improvement of Robert de Langton's Greek fire that he used to incinerate that slave vessel."

He carefully reached into the chest and removed one of the ceramic jars filled with a powder and a concoction known only to him. He had studied the remaining jars that Robert had left at his castle and was able to figure out the material that was in them that made them so combustible. He took a chance bringing them on the Green Ship, as they were extremely flammable, and all it would take would be a spark and the whole ship would explode. Therefore, he kept the chest locked and far away from the fire pit. He had made three of them and was reluctant to use them. The danger would have to be great but he saw how useful they had been when threatened by those pirate slavers. This was now an occasion where they might be extremely useful. He quickly unwrapped one of the wicks and pushed it through the paper into the jar. He looked up at Dagena.

"I hope that we don't need to use it, but I am going to be ready all the same."

She studied the jar with a dubious eye, but she had witnessed firsthand the effectiveness of the device when Robert had used it on the slavers ship. If Clement had made an improvement, it must be something remarkable and totally destructive. The boy was smarter than anyone that she had ever met and that included all the adults in her world. Of course, she was no dummy herself, and often took pride in giving him ideas which he took and utilized with great effectiveness. She was about to give him one of those ideas when their attention was arrested by a commotion and loud voices out on the deck.

"That's the Black Ship! Look at the size of that thing!" someone shouted. It sounded like Trousett.

Clement and Dagena raced out onto the deck and found Trousett standing with Pierre, Jacques and the men-at-arms leaning against the port rail. About two hundred yards in the distance Clement noticed with horror what all the commotion was about. The Black Ship with Roger de Montfort on board was in a death struggle with a monster so large that it seemed like something only talked about in tall tales. The leviathan had wrapped some of its long sinewy tentacles around the hull of the vessel. One of the larger arms had turned itself around the mast and was rocking the ship back and forth while frantic men could be seen smashing and slashing at it with axes and swords. The main body and head of the creature was still half submerged in the water, but Clement could see its two dark soulless eyes and for a few seconds stood frozen, almost paralyzed by their hypnotic glare.

"We have to get closer!" Clement exclaimed loudly.

"Closer? Are...are you mad sire?" Trousett asked in a panicked tone. "That thing will drag us into the abyss along with it!"

"We must help them!"

Clement rushed toward the tiller but found Gorm already there. He was relieving the less experienced mariner who had been working it.

"I shall get us close me lord!"

Thinking quickly, Clement ordered Jacques and the men-at arms to arm themselves with battle axes instead of swords, but the giant had already thought of it. They stood at the rail watching helplessly as the massive leviathan violently shook the Black Ship. Men were scattered about the deck attempting to keep their balance and at the same time chop at the massive tubular arms of the creature.

"Oh god!" Alice screamed. "I can't look!" She buried her head in Olaf's shoulder and began to weep.

One of the kraken's long scaly green arms had turned itself around one of the men and had lifted him high into the hazy sky. The man was thrashing about violently attempting to wrest himself from the creature's grasp, but finally and violently, the arm with the man still held captive to it, slammed down into the icy, churning sea. When it reappeared, the man was gone.

Gorm skillfully maneuvered the Green Ship closer to the troubled vessel which was listing at a dangerous angle to port. Some of the men had slid into the ocean while others were clinging to anything that they could hold onto in a desperate effort to survive. Clement ordered Esteban and the archers to hold their shots until the Green Ship was in effective range, but before they could get off an attack a tremendous crack was heard that reverberated into the stillness of the afternoon. Shockingly, the Black Ship split into two pieces, the mast jerking violently from the hold came down with a tremendous crash into the sea. In desperation, Esteban ordered the archers to attack and a flurry of arrows issued forth from atop the sterncastle. They were still too far away for the missiles to have any effect on the monster and only half of them hit their mark, bouncing harmlessly off the scaly flesh, the rest of them landing in the sea. They watched in sheer horror as the bow of the Black Ship slid beneath the surface of the water. The stern quickly began to fill with icy sea water, and for a short time it lingered on the surface as the monster's arms held it fast. Clement could see Roger de Montfort heroically straddling the tiller slashing at one of the grotesque arms with his sword, until, in one final pull, the creature slid beneath the surface dragging Sir Roger and the remaining part of the hull with it to a watery grave.

The water became quiet. Only a white foam with scattered bubbles told the tale of where the Black Ship last sailed. Clement could see Ceres and the Red Ship, sail furled and men furiously manning the oars heading in their direction. The Brown Ship with Sir William on board was still far away off starboard. He seemed to be in no hurry to lend any sort of assistance. A few of Sir Roger's men could be seen struggling in the icy water, but by the time that the Green Ship arrived they too had succumbed to the frigid temperatures, only one man was plucked from the sea by the crew of the Red Ship, the sole survivor of the kraken's fury.

They stood at the rail staring helplessly at the spot where the monster had submerged. Clement had gathered his bow and quiver and dragged the chest with the incendiary devices out onto the deck. It would be their only chance if the creature returned. For a few minutes there was silence. Clement could see Ceres standing on the bow of the Red Ship armed with a long sharp spear and that gave him an idea.

"Someone go below and fetch me a harpoon," he ordered to no one in particular. There was a rush of activity as men desperate for any sort of confidence in leadership acted on impulse to obey the order. It was Trousett who presented the young count with the weapon.

"What are you going to do?" he asked fearfully.

"I'm going to destroy this beast if it should show itself again," he said with a cool head.

Clement took the harpoon and kneeled on the deck in front of his chest. A crowd of people gathered around him to see what he was up to. They watched him carefully pull out one of the ceramic jars and then a coil of hemp. He tied the hemp around the slim iron handle on the jar and then loop it through the hole at the end of the lance where normally a rope would be attached to prevent the harpoon from slipping through the hunter's fingers. He then firmly bound the jar around the harpoon with more hemp and stood up. He turned to Olaf.

"Have a torch ready."

His friend did not hesitate and a minute later returned from the sterncastle holding the burning cresset aloft. They waited patiently and in silence. Suddenly there was a shout from the Red Ship. Ceres was pointing at a spot near the bow of the Green Ship. There was a scream and then shouts and when Clement turned he was shocked at what he saw. A massive green scaly arm had reached out of the sea and scooped Dagena up into the sky. Her eyes wide in terror, her mouth open but unable to utter any sound as fear had gripped her to the bone.

Chapter 11

lement acted swiftly and instinctively while Dagena thrashed helplessly in the monster's grip. The large green arm with its slimy circular suction cups held her fast, swinging her haphazardly across the sky, sometimes coming dangerously close to smashing her against the mast. The other arms had encircled the Green Ship in a death hold, the strong timbers straining against the leviathan's strength. They gently pulled the hard body of the creature up the hull of the vessel and Clement could see its dark, forbidding eyes appearing like craters to hell.

"Light the wick Olaf! Hurry!" Clement screamed.

Olaf, shaking with tension, performed the task and handed the cresset to Alice before taking his sword and plunging it into the tentacle that was holding Dagena captive. Clement knew that he only had seconds before the jar in his hands exploded and if he mistimed it, he, along with the rest of the Green Ship would be reduced to atoms. Climbing to the top of the sterncastle, he lifted himself up and steadied himself on one of the merlons. He was gripping the harpoon tightly. He could see Jacques and Pierre hacking at the arm that held Dagena prisoner. He did not hesitate. He had to save her. It was his only thought. The risk to himself was a moot point. If he died in the attempt, so be it. The mantle of the creature was slowly inching up the hull. Clement knew that he had only one chance and he took it. He leaped through the air and landed on the back of the kraken plunging the harpoon into one of its eyes. What happened next, he remembered only in a fog. He slid down the thrashing creature's slimy mantle and found himself plunging into the icy sea. His body almost immediately went into hypothermic shock and he found himself slipping downward into the salty black depths. And then... it came, a loud explosion. He felt strangely calm and warm as his body was propelled upward toward the light. The last thing that he remembered before blacking out was seeing the massive form of Adam leaping into the water.

Voices, faint and distant. Clement could hear mumbling... familiar sounds. He felt something rubbing his hands, feet and chest. He could see the ceiling of the sterncastle, but only through a long narrow tunnel. He felt as if he were in another far-off world, ethereal and distant. He was helpless to do anything except let time take its course. He tried to speak, but only syllables issued forth into the chilly air.

"He's coming back to us!" he heard someone exclaim. It was Olaf.

"Keep the circulation going! He's drifting in and out!" came another voice. It was Alice.

Clement's mind was racing. Random thoughts floating in and out, confusion and turmoil. He saw his father in a sunny field, the dandelions in full bloom. Count Hugo, dressed in black burnished chain mail. He was smiling and standing next to a pleasant looking young lady with long golden hair that seemed to radiate like the sun. He knew that this was his mother, though he had never met her. She was smiling also, but at the same time seemed to be sad, as if she wanted to say something to him.

"F...father? M...mother?"

He was mumbling incoherently. His teeth chattering violently. A trickle of blood formed at the corner of his mouth and he heard a voice.

"Hold his jaw! He is going to bite his tongue off!" Osment screamed.

Olaf pulled down on his chin and Osment forced a piece of wood between his teeth. Clement thrashed about violently as Pierre and Baldwin wrapped his cold shivering body in a warm wool blanket while Jacques pinned his legs down. After a few minutes he felt himself relaxing and then became still. He was still in the sunny field, but it started to fade. His parents were still smiling but they seemed to be moving away from him. Then reality hit him. With a sudden burst of strength and energy he bolted upright, ejecting the wood from his mouth.

"Dagena! Dagena! Oh, where art thou!"

He was still looking through a tunnel when they gently forced him back down on the mattress that they had dragged over next to the fire. Suddenly, a face appeared, hovering over him, her fiery red hair and fine features shining brilliantly in the glow of the fire.

"I...I am here Clement. Did you think that a wicked old kraken could snuff the life out of me? You know me better than that!"

She leaned forward and cradled his head in her lap, gently stroking his long wet, blond locks.

"Oh! Oh! Dagena it is you!" Is all that he could think to say. His face showing confusion as he attempted to gather his thoughts.

"Where.... where is the kraken? D...did I kill it?"

"Uh, yes, Clement. Its guts and flesh are scattered all over the deck thanks to you. And this is getting to be a habit of yours, first you kill a despotic king and now a beast from the deep!"

"Ha!" Olaf exclaimed proudly. "Clement is a hero, like St. George slaying the dragon! I've never seen anything like it!"

Clement closed his eyes and smiled as Dagena ran her long slender fingers through his hair.

"I...I'm no hero," he said modestly. "If I didn't have my friends, why...why I would be nothing."

He was still shivering mildly and Dagena wrapped the blanket tighter around his shoulders.

Olaf stood up and breathed a sigh of relief.

"Well, that was scary, but time for me to get to work, Clement," he said.

"Work?" Clement asked, his eyes fluttering.

"We are off course. It is almost night and we are heading away from the sun. We should be heading towards it."

Clement was now wide awake.

"Help me up, I need to take a reading with the Astrolabe," he said, before realizing that he was not wearing a stitch of clothing.

"Oh! Oh! someone, fetch me a robe," he said, embarrassed. It was at this point that he suddenly thought about Adam.

"I was saved by Adam! Where is he?"

There was a hushed silence that fell over the cabin. Clement, who was now sitting up, glanced around him suspiciously.

"Where is Adam? I ask again!"

He started shaking again. Dagena threw a robe over his bare shoulders. Her face showed sadness. He searched the faces around him and they all told him the same thing. He felt his eyes watering and his mouth began to quiver. He quickly buried his head in his hands and sobbed while Dagena tried to console him. She sent everyone else out, and for a few minutes they just held each other.

"He...he lifted you out of the water Clement and swam with you on his back until Jacques threw him a rope. He tied it around you and you were hauled unconscious onto the deck. When he went to throw Adam the rope he was gone. He never resurfaced Clement."

Clement finally lifted his head. He was still shivering, his face red and tear streaked.

"Did anyone try searching the water for him?" he asked desperately.

"Yes, but it was chaos for a while. When that monster exploded, the arm that was clutching me went limp and luckily was only a few feet off the deck or I would have been in the water too. That other kraken is still out there somewhere, Clement. Olaf has all hands-on deck searching for it in case it should appear."

Clement wiped his eyes and then looked serious.

"Dagena, I saw that thing grab you...I had to do something."

She smiled. "You saved everyone on this ship Clement. It is not your fault that Adam is gone. It was God's will for him to come into our lives and save you. Don't you see that?"

He was biting his bottom lip and for the first time noticed that his tongue hurt from biting it.

"Dagena, can you go in my chest and get me a new shirt, pair of breeches and stockings. I'll throw that old wool coat over my shoulders until my cloak is dry."

It was then that he noticed the condition of her heavy gown and a hint of a smile broke out on his face.

"Dagena, one more thing."

She was heading towards his chest but turned with a curious expression.

"You might want to change into your spare gown, ha! ha! you've been slimed!"

Horrified, she reached around her back and immediately felt the oily liquid stuck to her. She looked at her hand in disgust.

"Ooh! And it smells too!" she screamed in disgust, wrinkling her nose. "You will have to wait for me to get your clothes Clement! When it comes to appearance, I come first!"

Clement burst out laughing, temporarily forgetting Adam, but trying to lighten the mood which had become melancholic. He looked at his hands and feet and noticed how cold and blue they looked. He suddenly wondered how they could still function. He should be dead, but here he was sitting next to a small fire, still shivering, trying to stay warm. He felt happy, but sad at the same time. He could hear the hustle and bustle of activity outside. They would be scouring the deck and cleaning the vessel from the mess that he had made but they were undoubtedly happy that he had made it. He suddenly wondered why he had been the one tasked with all this responsibility. Why him? Sure, his noble birth was part of the reason. After all, he was a descendant of Rollo and King Harold Godwinson, But why him? His father should still be alive. If Hugo had not died, would he even be on this ship? Probably not. He would not have scored a great martial victory over his uncle Sven the Terrible, therefore King Henry would never have heard of him. His reputation as the boy knight who saved the commoner from a tyrannical warlord would not exist. He would be just some obnoxious, anonymous boy heir that would be out playing with his hawk and studying the art of war. That was another thing that bothered him. Why did there have to be war? He hated war, but, unfortunately for him, he happened to be good at it. He had destroyed his cruel uncle's army and rid the land of the tyrant robber known as le Diable. Now, here he was killing tyrannical kings and krakens. What next?

Dagena took her time changing and when she returned, Clement had noticed that she had donned her thick green gown and was rummaging through his chest. She handed him his clothes and sat down next to him. He tried to be discreet behind the wool blanket while he dressed. He heard Dagena laughing.

"Why are you laughing Dagena?"

"Because you look ridiculous sitting under that blanket putting those breeches on."

He dropped the blanket so that she could only see his blond head poking out above it. He still looked cold and miserable but he was smiling and was slowly recovering from the shock of the frigid water.

"Maybe, I'll just sit here for a little while Dagena. Won't you come sit next to me?"

She was washing her hands in a pail of water sprinkled with cloves and when she was done, dried them on her gown.

"I do hope that I no longer smell like fish," she said, sitting down next to him. He leaned towards her and breathed deeply with his nose in an exaggerated manner. She noticed that he had a devilish look on his face and when he went to say something, she stopped him by playfully rapping his skull with her thumb like she usually did. He laughed but then became serious again, lowering his head.

"Dagena, I...well...I hope I know what I am doing. Do you think that I am doing right?"

He looked at her and she could see the worry on his face.

"I don't understand," she replied. "Doing right about what?"

"Continuing onward," he said softly. "It is such a worrisome thing to have all these people relying on you to make the right decisions. We had four ships. Now we have three. That is my fault."

She reached over and grabbed his one hand that was sticking out beyond the blanket.

"Your fault? How could you have stopped that kraken from doing what its instincts tell it to do? You alone saved this ship Clement!"

She leaned forward and kissed him on the cheek. He was about to do the same when there suddenly arose a clatter of voices and shouts from the deck.

"It's Adam!" Osment screamed.

Clement and Dagena both burst out the door. They could see everyone standing at the port rail. Adjacent to and almost parallel to the Green Ship, the Red Ship sailed calmly in the light breeze about 200 yards away. Standing near the rail was the unmistakable form of Adam wrapped in a warm blanket standing next to Ceres the Greek who was waving happily at them. Clement suddenly felt elated and his energy soar. If there

had been any residue left of his previous condition,
it had now disappeared.

Chapter 12

The days passed by and for the most part they were uneventful. A routine on board the Green Ship became the norm. Everyone went about their duty, some getting restless. Clement plotted the course the best he could manage, using his astrolabe with skill and jotting down the readings in his logbook. He had even given classes to some of the others in case he should become disabled or die. He tried not to think of this, but already, he had almost died twice on this voyage, so it was worth preparing for that possibility. They had seen the other kraken a few times. At least they believed that it was the same one. It was not as big as the one that Clement had destroyed, and hardly looked capable of crushing the Green Ship, but who knew what other monsters lurked beneath these depths. A few times they had spotted large whales, some of them blowing a watery mist into the air which Osment took note of and correctly ascertained the reason for it. After discussing the possibilities with Clement and Dagena he came to a firm conclusion. They had no gills and needed to come to the surface to breathe. Trousett had once had the opportunity to examine a dead one and confirmed this logic.

They were now entering the sea of giant ice crystals. Some of them gigantic in size. White and blue, they glistened in the sunshine and if one looked at them for too long with the sun shining on them, they were temporarily blinded. At night Clement ordered the vessels to fire up their oil lamps and hang them from hooks attached to the rails to light the way. He did not want to risk one of his ships striking one which could lead to disastrous consequences. He had stored vats of olive oil in the hull and he was glad that he had the foresight to do this. He kept a man constantly on duty to monitor the lamps. Fire was always a danger at sea.

It had been weeks since anyone had seen land and there was some grumbling among some of the men, especially on the Brown Ship which was continuously signaling them. Sir William was getting impatient and had reservations regarding Clement's navigational ability. Clement continued to check his readings and had plotted his course accordingly. He surmised that they were nearing the coast of the old Norse settlements, but he was worried that he might be sailing too far to the south and would miss the land entirely. Supplies were still in good order but they were running low on their supply of fresh water, as some of the casks had become contaminated. Osment estimated that they had at least a three-week supply if they consumed it at their current rate, so Clement cut the ration in half. It was still more than enough. They still had plenty of wine. A few men had gotten sick, including Trousett who seemed to be suffering from the scurvy. Osment treated him and the others with a twice daily dose of chicory water and wine and slowly they seemed to come around. Dagena, too, had taken an interest in Osment's medical experiments and became quite efficient at preparing the cures.

Sometimes, Adam would appear on the deck of the Red Ship and wave and holler at the crew of the Green Ship who would always wave back. Clement wondered how he could have survived the frigid temperatures of the ocean and somehow, miraculously, be hauled aboard the Red Ship seemingly none worse for the wear. It seemed impossible, yet he was living proof that it had happened. Sir William in the Brown Ship seemed aloof and as usual kept a distance from the other two vessels, sometimes vanishing from view. At one point the Brown Ship completely disappeared for almost two days. The crew of the Green Ship thought them lost, but on the morning of the third day, there it was, clinging to the horizon. Clement did not know if Sir William was doing this intentionally, or merely having trouble keeping up.

About ten days after the encounter with the kraken, a shout was heard from the crow's nest.

"Land! Starboard!"

"Are you sure that it is not ice?" Clement yelled back.

"Nay, tis land for sure!"

"Man the oars!"

Clement could barely hear his own voice as the wind was whipping across the deck, but he began barking orders to the crew. One of Gorm's sailors was at the tiller and soon had the Green Ship rolling along in the choppy sea in the direction of the land. Olaf hurried below deck and ordered the rowers to steer starboard. It was mid-afternoon and although the days were short because of their latitude, they hoped to narrow the distance to land before night set in.

"Tis the land of the Norseman," Baldwin said, with Bran at his heels.

The dog began to bark and the reason was soon ascertained. A large fulmar with its grey wings and white protruding belly was gliding majestically over the ship. It seemed to be inquisitively observing the strange vessel. Soon, another one appeared in the sky and the closer the ship moved toward land the more prevalent they became. Finally, some of them were boldly landing on the mast.

"I've never seen a gull like that," Dagena said with amazement.

"Neither have I. Perhaps they are giving us a welcome!" Clement said.

After a while, the wind shifted against them and Clement ordered the sail furled and a constant rotation of men at the oars. Jacques kept the men at the oars motivated by singing songs in his loud but harmonious voice and even took his turn pulling. After a few hours of constant, brutal work, the Green Ship found itself in a small bay. It was nearly dark and the shoreline looked bleak and foreboding, a windswept landscape, with rocky patches of dead grass mixed with snow. From the top of the sterncastle, Clement studied the terrain with his glass, but it was too dark to see much of anything. He handed it to Dagena and she quickly grabbed him by the shoulder.

"Look! Clement, do you see it?"

"See what?"

She was pointing toward an outcrop of rocks piled together on the lonely beach. Taking back the glass he caught a glimpse of something white and hairy scurrying behind a boulder. Whatever it was, it appeared to be massive in size. He waited patiently; the glass still held to his eye.

"Sire, we took a sounding as you requested, we are at 20 fathoms," Pierre yelled from the deck.

Clement lowered the glass.

"Thanks Pierre, lower the anchors!"

He turned to Dagena who was still looking at the desolate spot on the beach where she had seen the mysterious looking creature.

"What do you think that thing was?"

He shrugged. "I don't know Dagena, it looked like a bear, but not any kind that I have ever seen or heard of."

"You've seen a bear before?"

"Yes, my father and I encountered one in the forest one morning. It was using its paws to catch fish in the river. It did not bother us, and we did not bother it, but merely kept our distance from it. I do not think that this thing is a bear Dagena."

Clement ordered the oil lamps lit and it was soon dark. The Red Ship had anchored within hailing distance from them and the Brown Ship at the mouth of the bay. It was an eerily quiet night and so cold that the men not on watch huddled in their blankets below deck to keep warm. Alice was having a particularly rough time and spent most of the time in the sterncastle huddled around the small fire with Dagena, Clement, Olaf and Osment.

"We are getting low on wood for fuel," Osment said, blowing into his hands. "And I did not see any trees, perhaps we might explore some of these inlets and fjords and see where they lead."

"That is a good idea Osment," Clement said. "We will take the skiff out in the morning and see what we can find."

Dagena made a funny face. "Well, I should say, that I do not want to encounter that strange looking beast that we saw earlier."

"Well, this is a strange and different land. There is no telling what we might encounter," Clement replied. "But we will be armed and prepared for any trouble."

Suddenly, there was a loud wailing sound coming from the direction of the shore. It was unlike anything that any of them had ever heard before. In the stillness of the night, it was even more startling. Alice nudged closer to Olaf and the five teens could almost hear their hearts beating in their chests. It was unnerving and then it happened again. This time even louder.

"What...what is that?" Alice asked nervously.

"Shh! There it goes again," Dagena responded.

For a minute, all ears listened carefully. They could hear the guard shuffling about nervously on the deck, but the eerie cry was not heard again.

In the morning, at first light, Clement gave the order to pull anchors and the fleet sailed out of the bay and began its exploration of the coast. Within a short time, they discovered an inlet and took a sounding. They were still at 20 fathoms, but as they entered the inlet the water became shallower until Clement decided to not risk going any further. He was afraid that they might hit a sandbar or rocks. They could see snow covered mountains with a little shrubbery but no trees. Clement decided that they could haul some wood and replenish their water there. He ordered both skiffs lowered and a barge to tow the wood and water barrels. The water was cold with a thin layer of ice along the shore. They would have to be extremely careful when landing. Clement attempted to dissuade Dagena from coming along, but of course she was adamant about getting off the ship as was Olaf and Alice. They piled into the smaller skiff with Gorm, Esteban and Pierre, while Osment, Trousett and 8 men-at-arms and archers gathered in the larger boat with most of the gear.

Baldwin and Jacques remained on the ship with the sailors. The Red Ship also lowered a boat. Clement was happy to see Adam sitting in the back, helping to row with 5 other men including Ceres. Clement had also signaled the Brown Ship, but Sir William responded that he would be delayed and to go forward without him.

The three boats rowed skillfully through a narrow fjord avoiding large chunks of broken ice that floated in the water in irregular patches. They were looking for a spot to land, a beachhead where they could construct a base camp and then make hikes into the interior to find water and wood. On both sides of them were towering grey cliffs, in some places, covered with a dead moss and ice. Finally, after a few miles they found what they were looking for. The beach was small, but there was a place where they could land and set up camp, before trekking across the snow-covered rocks.

They had pulled their boats up onto the beach and the men set to work erecting the three tents that they had brought with them. It might be a few days until they returned and they would have to protect themselves from the harsh weather of this climate at night if they were to be successful. They had stacked the barrels on the raft and rolled them up onto the beach and quickly finished setting up camp. It was agreed that Ceres and his men, along with Gorm would stay and man the camp, while the rest went off to search for fresh water and wood. Clement broke the men up into three search parties. He would lead the first one, Trousett would lead the second and Pierre would lead the third. Osment would remain behind at camp and act as a doctor, with Alice assisting him in case anyone required attention. Clement, of course, took Dagena and Olaf with him along with Adam and Esteban. They started up a steep incline that soon leveled off and then dropped down into a large spacious valley enclosed within a mountain range.

"This is a barren wasteland," Olaf said. "I doubt that we will find anything larger than these small shrubs."

Dagena felt the small narrow leaves which were covered by a white, downy fuzz.

"It looks to be a type of willow tree," Clement said. "I would say that this land is uninhabited. I thought that it might be the location of the Norse colony, but I do not see how anyone could possibly live here."

"Well sire, you would be wrong!" Esteban exclaimed from the top of a small hillock. "Look yonder!"

They rushed over to where Esteban was standing and for a few seconds stood there gazing at the scene in wonderment. A long stone structure was plainly visible further down in the valley among the thick brambles and willows that posed as a forest in this inhospitable place.

"I think that we should go back and get the others," Olaf said.

Clement shook his head and pondered Olaf's suggestion.

"It is a ruin, Olaf. Look at the condition of the roof. Timbers have collapsed. Nobody has lived there for years."

They slowly crept forward until Adam in his excitement broke out into a run down the snowy slope.

"A house! A house!"

Clement cupped his hands together around his mouth. "Adam come back!"

Adam either ignored him or did not hear him and the big boy soon disappeared around the corner of the stone structure, his arms flapping wildly with excitement. They hurried down the slope, all caution thrown to the wind. They need not have worried, for the structure was abandoned as Clement had told them. Small weeds and tall dead brown grass had invaded the old house, which had been built in the style of an old Norse longhouse. The timber beams that supported the arched roof were still visible, but had collapsed into the structure, some of them still notched together.

"Now this is puzzling," Dagena said thoughtfully.

"What is?" Clement asked.

"Well, those timbers for one. Where did they come from? Certainly not from around here Clement. Do you see any trees larger than these small shrubs?"

Clement studied one of the beams.

"You are right Dagena. This wood is oak. They must have been carried in from the ships, or there is another forest around here that we have yet to discover. I am betting on the ships."

"But where are the people?" Olaf asked. "There is nothing around here but dead shrubs, rocks and snow."

"I do not know," Clement said. "But they were here at one time, and they left us these old timbers. There is enough wood here to last us for a while. We can have a bonfire tonight at the camp."

"Fresh water!"

They turned to see Esteban waving at them from an outcrop of rocks, and quickly made their way to him.

"We will have to chip the ice away, but this spring will provide us with all we should need."

"Great work Esteban! We can head back to camp and bring the sled back with the barrels at first light and gather these timbers. We can drag a few of them back and make a fire tonight."

They returned to find that Pierre was already back and had also found some fresh water, but no wood. It was just getting dark. Ceres and Gorm had started a fire using willow branches and they were overjoyed when they saw Adam with four large timbers on his shoulders and Esteban and Olaf carrying one.

"Where the devil did ye find those timbers sire?" Gorm asked happily. "We broke up a bunch of these dead willow branches. That's all we could find."

Clement related the discovery of the old Norse longhouse and the spring.

"Well, my lord, this will get us through this cold night," Ceres said. "Have you seen Trousett and the others?"

"Nay," Clement answered. "The last we saw of them was when they disappeared along that ridge line to the east of us."

Ceres looked up toward the ridge. "Well, it is getting dark. If they do not come back soon, they shall almost certainly become lost."

Osment and Alice were preparing a few large salmon that one of Ceres men had caught and it was not long before they were handing out portions to everyone. Olaf had set up a roving guard of three men around the perimeter of the camp giving strict orders to keep a vigilant lookout for anything out of the ordinary. As the evening grew later, Clement began to worry about Trousett and the four men that he had with him. They should have been back long ago. He had told everyone to be back before darkness.

"I think that we should probably send out a search party for Trousett. They should have been back hours ago," Olaf said, sipping on a mug full of chicory water.

Clement shook his head. Staring into the hypnotic flames, all eyes were on him as he pondered Olaf's suggestion.

"And risk having more people lost in the darkness? No Olaf, they will have to manage by themselves tonight. They are dressed warmly enough. I am worried about them though. Trousett is not one to take unnecessary risks."

Olaf shrugged.

"I see your logic sire, but what if Dagena, or Alice was out there in the darkness. What then?"

"But they are not out there Olaf. That would change everything. I would be the first one out there searching, but these are men that are lost, not girls."

Clement felt a swat on the back of his head which nearly took his wool cap off. He turned to see Dagena glaring at him with her arms folded, a wide smirk on her cherubic face.

"We are just girls huh? So, you don't think that we can take care of ourselves like you boys?"

Clement rolled his eyes and glanced at Olaf who was chuckling.

"Now Dagena, I did not mean that you…"

He never finished his sentence but was interrupted by a hideous wailing sound that penetrated the cold air somewhere in the distance. Dagena practically jumped into Clement's lap, grabbing him around the neck, causing him to spill his chicory water.

"Oh my god! what was that?" she screamed. He started to stand up, Dagena still clinging to him.

"Uh...Dagena," he said, trying to get his balance.

She let go when they almost toppled over. She then started laughing at her ridiculous behavior. He could not help but shake his head and smile, but the humor was short lived when the wailing sound was suddenly heard again, this time much louder and followed by the unmistakable cry of a human voice screaming in sheer agony. Clement reached for his bow while everyone else gathered up their weapons.

"That is the same sound we heard last evening," Alice said sharply.

"But without that cry of terror," Olaf added. "I wonder if it was from Trousett's party?"

"It's a banshee!" Someone yelled. "That means that someone in this camp will die tonight!"

"I say we get on the boats and row back this evening. This place is cursed!" someone else said.

Clement held up his arm.

"That's enough! That talk is superstitious rubbish. Whatever that thing is out there it bleeds just like we do."

"But what is it sire? It surely is not human," the first voice asked. He was one of Ceres men, a sailor with a thick brown beard.

Gorm stepped into the light of the campfire. His old eyes weary, but at the same time sparkling. No one said a word, as they all knew that Gorm had seen just about everything in his more than 70 years of life.

"I will tell ye what it is, but ye all must remain calm and listen to the wise counsel of his lordship."

Clement swallowed and his eyes became big, knowing that they were about to hear one of Gorm's tales.

"When I was a youth, I knew an old Norseman whose grandfather had sailed with Leif Eriksson to a land west of here, where the trees grow in great abundance and strange creatures dwell, some with horns, others twice the size of bears. These beasts roam the land in herds of thousands. There is a pigeon whose flocks are so large that they blot out the sun! But none of these peculiar and odd monstrosities can compare to something that is said to live in the bowels of the earth and come forth into the open air only at twilight!"

"What…what is it?" Alice asked anxiously. She felt her heart beating rapidly and gripped Olaf's hand tightly.

"Aye my lady. I am about to tell ye. Tis a hairy monster on two legs that stands six to seven cubits at the shoulders! Some be white and some brown with eyes dark and soulless! Nothing can stand up to it, but it is said to fear man and is elusive by nature!"

As Gorm uttered these words, the wailing sound was heard again and seemed to echo into the valley beyond them.

"This…this longhouse that we found today," Clement said softly. "It has been abandoned for years. I wonder if these creatures had anything to do with the disappearance of these settlers?"

"Perhaps," Gorm said ominously. "Sire, It would be wise to double the watch and keep the fire burning all night."

"Gorm, your counsel is wise and shall be heeded."

Clement turned to Ceres and Pierre who were standing with their arms folded across the fire from them.

"Ceres, your men will take the first watch. I want the men to rove the perimeter of the camp in pairs. Pierre, you will take our men and keep the second watch."

"What about me sire?" Gorm asked dutifully.

"You?"

Clement put his hand on the old man's shoulder.

"You will turn in for the night my friend. You are old and though strong we need your wise counsel to be fresh and it cannot be impeded by lack of sleep."

"But my duty, I..."

Clement interrupted him.

"That is not a request Gorm," he said with a quirky smile.

"Aye me lord. I suppose I am rather tired, but if ye need me ye know where to find me."

With that said, Gorm turned and entered the largest of the three tents, the flap closing behind him. Within a few minutes the camp had become quiet. Dagena and Alice had entered the smallest tent that had been brought along just for the girls.

"I don't like it Clement," Olaf said, shivering slightly with the cold. "Those girls being in their all by themselves with that creature lurking about. I'm going to sit out in front of their tent all night."

He unsheathed his sword and sat down with it across his lap in front of the girl's tent. Clement and Osment looked at each other, each boy not wanting to look bad by Olaf's chivalric gesture.

"Well, if you are going to sit out here all night, so am I," Clement said, shrugging his shoulders and sitting down next to Olaf with his bow across his lap. Not to be outdone, Osment shook his head and sat down next to them. For a few moments, the three boys merely sat there in silence until Olaf began humming a tune. Clement and Osment soon joined him in this merriment. Suddenly, an angry head with flowing red hair poked out of the flap. All three heads turned at once to see Dagena showing them her fist.

"I don't care if you three boys sit out here all night but the next one that utters a sound is going to get this square across the jaw!"

They heard Alice laughing from inside and Dagena's head disappeared back into the confines of the tent. The boys looked at one another and began laughing, however, being careful to keep it so low that they would not feel the wrath of the red-haired girl.

The inky darkness of the night wore on and one by one Clement, Olaf and Osment drifted off to sleep on the bare ground, wrapped in their warm heavy cloaks. It was shortly before sunrise when Clement awoke to the sound of a blood curdling scream that resonated through the shadowy light of the early morning.

Chapter 13

agena and Alice flew out of the tent to find Osment all alone, dagger in hand, standing in front of the tent flap.

Dagena scanned the morning dawn and then turned to Osment.

"Where is Clement?"

He told me to stay here and watch you girls. He and Olaf are leading a party to investigate the scream. It might be Trousett or one of his men."

"Are we all alone?" Alice asked.

"No, Ceres and his men are here with us. He gave them strict instructions to stay in camp."

Dagena brushed by him and ran toward the fire, where she found Ceres talking with Gorm and one of his men.

"Which way did he go?"

Ceres looked befuddled, but it was Gorm who tried to calm her.

"Now, my lady, his lordship knows what is right. Ye will stay in camp with us and we will make certain no harm comes to ye."

"Gorm, I am not worried about harm coming to me! It is Clement that I am worried about. He is rash and impetuous sometimes."

Alice and Osment joined them around the fire. Ceres had his four men roving around the perimeter of the camp in pairs. Dagena thought about the strange creature that she and Clement had seen from the deck of the Green Ship. Was this the same type of beast that Gorm had told them about? Was it also the source of the strange wailing sounds and screams that they had been hearing throughout the night?

She was about to ask Gorm his thoughts on the matter when suddenly the eerie sound was heard again. It seemed much closer. Osment immediately pivoted around toward the direction of the cry, clutching his dagger tightly. Ceres had drawn his sword from his scabbard and stood between the direction of the sound and Alice. Dagena had disappeared and, when she returned, she was holding a bow and strapping a quiver to her waist.

"If it comes into this camp, I'll be ready," she said bravely.

Gorm cleared his throat and took a swig of water from his horn.

"It will not harm us, my lady," he said. "It fears us more than we fear it."

"Gorm, you might be right, but I, for one, am not going to take any chances."

They waited for what seemed an eternity, the wailing cry breaking the silence every few minutes. Finally, voices could be heard and then shadowy forms appeared on the crest of the hill, moving over it and down towards them. Ceres immediately called in his roving guard, who took up a defensive position around the fire until they determined it was Clement and Olaf returning with the others, including one of Trousett's men who was caked with blood and had a white cloth tied around his head.

"What the devil happened?" Osment asked, placing his dagger back in his sheath.

"I will let him explain," Clement said, pointing to the injured man, who was brought to the fire. He was a large man with a thick blond beard. Dagena recognized him as one of the highly capable men-at-arms on the Green Ship and knew his name only as Drago.

Alice had brewed some chicory water and handed the bloodied man a mug full.

"Oh, my lady, I thank thee!" he said, bringing the hot mug up to his cracked and weathered lips.

"We lost ourselves in the darkness out on the ridge," he said quietly. "Aye, we sat down to rest and then heard something moving below us, among the rocks. Then, it appeared! The largest two-legged creature I have ever seen. It stood nearly twice the size of a man! It was naked, covered with white hair, the color of the snow! But the eyes! Aye, the eyes! They were black and glassy, demonic looking! We were frightened out of our wits and could do nothing but stare at it in the moonlight! It was as if we had entered a state of enchantment. It stood there looking at us. Trousett finally broke his gaze and ordered us to attack it. We did so, reluctantly, fearing for our lives. I saw the monster lift Trousett up over his shoulders and hurl him through the air, over the side of the cliff as if he were no heavier than a young girl's rag doll. Then the beast broke James into two pieces and crushed Stephen's bones in a powerful grip! I started to run for my life, and while I was running, I heard Hubert cry out in agony. I must have fallen and hit my head, for when I woke up, I was all alone. I was afraid to move in the dark, not knowing if the monster was lurking somewhere among the rocks. That is how his lordship found me! I am grateful to be alive! But my head, oh it does feel like it is on fire!"

Osment approached Drago and motioned for Alice to assist him.

"Come with us, Drago. We will patch you up."

The injured man disappeared into the largest tent, where Osment had his medical chest and an oil lamp.

"They attacked it, that is why they are dead," Gorm said sadly. "If they had left it alone, they would be here with us now."

"It is almost daylight," Clement said. "We will leave a strong guard here at the camp and the rest of us will drag the barrels down to that spring. It is not too far, but it will be painstaking work and take most of the day."

Breakfast was prepared and the two rafts were soon converted into a rolling cart with two small, thick wheels attached to it. Baldwin had designed it for just this purpose and Clement felt fortunate he had one of the finest carpenters in the world working for him. The morning sky in the east was pink, with ribbons of gray and purple. It was going to be a cold and dry day. Pierre was left in charge of the camp. With him, were two archers, along with Osment, Alice and Drago. The others would accompany Clement to the spring and gather more of the old timbers.

They arrived shortly and went to work while Clement, Dagena, and Olaf explored the Norse longhouse.

"I found something!" Dagena exclaimed with excitement. Clement and Olaf hurried over to her. She had been examining an old, weathered table with broken legs when she saw a sharp object protruding from the graveled floor.

"Looks like a dagger," said Olaf. Half of it had been buried and he pulled it out of the ground. The blade was rusty, but the ivory handle was in good condition. He handed it to Clement.

"What is that marking on it?" Dagena asked curiously. "It looks like a cross to me."

Clement turned it over in his hands.

"That's strange," he said mechanically.

Dagena looked puzzled. "What is?"

"The cross. It's a Templar cross."

"What's so strange about that?" Olaf inquired.

Clement's eyes narrowed and he became serious.

"What would a dagger with a cross of the Knights Templar be doing in this God forsaken place?"

Dagena shrugged. "I don't know. Maybe they were here trading with the Norse settlers."

"Why? Why would they want to do that?" Clement asked. "That makes absolutely no sense, Dagena. The Knights Templar have amassed wealth that King Henry could only dream of. Also, their primary mission is to protect the pilgrims on the road to the Holy Land. If they were here, they had some purpose for being here."

Dagena held up her finger. It was a eureka moment and she was smiling.

"Didn't King Henry mention a chest he wanted you to recover from this Sir Humphrey Rochford character?"

Clement looked puzzled.

"Yes. Why?"

"Did you ever think maybe Sir Humphrey does not have this chest but might be going to retrieve it? Perhaps, it is already there."

Clement thought about that for a few seconds and smiled.

"Dagena, you are a genius!"

She became animated. "Of course, I am, Clement!"

He was rubbing his chin and Dagena and Olaf knew what it meant. He was deep in thought.

"But if you are right. Why would anyone go to such lengths to bring this treasure, or whatever is in that chest, all the way to Vinland and then a few years later turn around and risk life and limb to retrieve it again...unless, of course, they were searching for something else. It doesn't add up."

Olaf asked to see the blade, and Clement handed it to him.

"Clement, the Templars might have brought this chest over but how do we know Sir Humphrey is a Templar? Perhaps King Louis and King Henry heard of this secret Templar voyage and that is why each of them has decided to send out an expedition to locate it."

Clement nodded. "Tis good logic, Olaf. We cannot assume this Sir Humphrey is a Templar. Maybe he is just a pawn of King Louis as I am being used as a pawn of King Henry. Well, no more, my good friends! Clement, Count of la Haye is no one's pawn! We will figure out this shady business and deal with it forthright!"

"Then we are still going to search for this place called Vinland?" Olaf asked. He was carefully examining the ivory handle of the blade.

"Of course, Olaf, and we shall find it!"

Suddenly there was a shout from the direction of the spring, and the three teens hurried to the location to find what all the hullabaloo was all about. Clement immediately discerned the cause. On the slope above the spring, Esteban had discovered some tracks in the snow. They were unlike anything anyone had ever seen, similar to a bear, but more like a human foot. The big toe being three times the size of the others.

"Sire, they disappear over the ridgeline," Esteban said.

Clement kneeled down to examine one of them and then looked up toward the ridge, a puzzled and worried look on his face.

"Let us finish up and get the water and timbers back to the camp. I do not like it."

For the next few hours, they worked hard. When they returned to the camp it was nearly dark. To Clement's surprise, he found Sir William standing around the blaze with three of his men talking to Pierre, Alice, and Osment. Alice rushed over to Olaf who tried to show her the blade that they had found, but she was more concerned for his welfare.

"I was worried about you, Olaf. It was starting to get dark and you had not returned."

He reached for her hand and they sat down on one of the large rocks near the fire.

"So! Looks like poor Trousett has met his maker…or maybe not!" Sir William exclaimed callously. He was chewing on a piece of smoked halibut, his eyes dark and penetrating.

Clement wanted to reach across the fire and strangle him but he maintained his calm demeanor and merely shrugged.

"Trousett was a good man, Sir William. He will be missed."

"Not by me, Clement de la Haye. That much is certain. He was a worthless scoundrel as far as I am concerned."

Sir William turned to one of his men and cackled at his own heartless comments. The man faked a laugh, an obsequious gesture. He wanted to please his superior. Clement was biting his tongue, not wanting to provoke the older man but Dagena was having none of it.

"You are crude and wicked to make such comments," she said. "A good man has died."

Sir William snickered and threw a fish bone into the fire.

"No one asked for your opinion, servant girl," he responded arrogantly.

Clement turned red in the face.

"Hold your tongue, sir! Or thou shall lose it!"

For a minute, no one said a word. Clement stood next to Dagena, glaring across the fire at Sir William, who chose to ignore his superiors' comment. He started to say something to one of his men, when the wailing sound, once again, penetrated the quietness of the night. It was the first time Sir William had heard it and it chilled him to the bone.

"What was that?" he asked nervously.

This time it was Gorm who started chuckling.

"That is the sound of the monster who killed Trousett. It would be wise if ye ignored it, Sir William."

"Ignore it?"

"Aye, sire. If ye ask me, that would be the prudent thing to do," Gorm added.

"Well, old man, I did not ask you. Now that everyone is here, it is time for me to tell you why I have suddenly decided to grace you with my presence on this dark, gloomy evening."

He glanced across the fire toward the boy count, who was standing with his arms folded, still glaring at him.

"And I address you, Count Clement, and no one else. From here on out, I am leader of this fleet. We are no longer sailing for King Henry. We now sail under the Fleur-de-lis of the King of France. While you were out here encountering this creature, or whatever it is, I took the liberty of securing the Red Ship in my name. Ceres, your services are no longer required, your men now belong to me."

He started cackling.

"Actually, they never belonged to you."

Sir William whistled loudly and suddenly a score of armed men appeared on the fringes of the camp. They had been lurking in the shadows after silently rowing to the shore a half mile to the south and furtively surrounding the camp. The men, who had been with Ceres, suddenly pulled out their daggers and stood with Sir William, who was rubbing his beard and condescendingly shaking his head at Clement. The boy count had pulled his dagger from his sheath as had Olaf, Pierre, and Esteban. Clement looked around desperately for his remaining five men, including Drago, but noticed with horror that they were nowhere to be found. Only Adam and Osment appeared, but both were being held with daggers against their necks.

"You treacherous dog!" Clement screamed.

"Ah! Such a vile mouth you have, Clement de la Haye," Sir William said with a wide grin. "For such a smart boy, I would have figured you would have taken greater precautions to secure your camp, but, then again, you had no idea I was acting under his majesty the King of France."

Clement boldly moved toward his antagonist, but Olaf, perceiving the danger, grabbed his arm.

"Where are my men?"

Sir William shrugged.

"It appears they have abandoned you, young count. Now, this is what is going to happen. I am not a cold-blooded murderer. I am a man of God as you shall see. Your remaining men, who stand with you around this warm hearth, will file into that small boat and paddle back to your vessel tonight, in the darkness, and, by the way, my men have already boarded it."

Clement felt himself becoming rigid with anger.

"That would be suicide in this darkness! We would almost certainly founder."

William frowned.

"Who said anything about WE! No, sir. You are to remain with me as a good faith hostage. I still need you to guide me to this land called Vinland."

Sir William snapped his fingers at one of his men.

"Disarm them and prepare the boat!"

Within a few seconds, Clement and his party had been disarmed, all except for Olaf who stubbornly refused to give up his sword. He stood standing next to Clement ready to plunge it into the first man who attempted to wrest it from him.

"Boy, if you do not give us your sword, I shall be forced to use it on you to strike your head off your scrawny body," Sir William said casually, as if he made the request every day.

Olaf stood his ground, glaring at their antagonist.

"Put it down, Olaf," Clement said quietly. "There is nothing you can do right now."

"I'll not, sire!"

"You will, Olaf. That's an order."

Reluctantly, the Danish boy threw his weapon on the ground without moving his eyes away from Sir William. If a stare could cut like a knife, Olaf's hatred would have slain Sir William on the spot. One by one, they were led into the boat, starting with Pierre, followed by Adam, Osment, Esteban, and Gorm. When it was time for them to lead Alice down to the boat, the man escorting her, pulled her roughly by the arm, when she hesitated to leave. Olaf had seen enough.

"Abuse a lady, do you! You cowardly heathen!"

He struck the bearded man across the face, knocking him down on the hard-packed snow. No sooner had he done so, he found himself hurled to the ground and set on by three of Sir William's men, one of whom sent a powerful fist crashing into his jaw, knocking him unconscious. Alice screamed and Clement immediately attempted to aid his friend, but he too found himself pinned to the ground by two burly henchmen and was soon bound, hand and foot, with ropes and unceremoniously thrown into one of the larger tents. Olaf was carried down to the boat, with Alice frantically trying to ascertain his condition.

The boat was soon cast away from the shore. Alice had managed to plead with Sir William for a few blankets and horns of water, which he begrudgingly granted her. Amidst all the chaos, Dagena had somehow managed to slip away in the darkness. They had completely forgotten about her. She refused to abandon Clement in this inhospitable place. Sir William had thought of nearly everything but, if there was one thing he did not count on, it was the resourceful nature and determined mind of a young girl, who, to him, was just a servant girl. She watched and waited...

Chapter 14

lement had landed inside the tent with a rough tumble. The burly brute, who had tossed him inside, had merely laughed before leaving him alone in the darkness. He could hear the ruckus outside and Alice's pleading, along with Sir William's gruff, gravelly voice as he barked orders and shouted commands at his subordinates. He could see the shadowy light of the fire against the side of the tent and hear the crackling popping sound of wood, but he was too far away to feel its warmth. For a short time, he struggled against the ropes that held him fast but succeeded in doing nothing except rolling around and chafing his wrists until they started to bleed. Finally, he quit struggling and became still. He needed to think. He had to use his mind to extricate himself from this precarious predicament. He knew his life was not in danger. Sir William needed him to get to Vinland. He was the only one with the knowledge and skills to get them there. However, it was not himself he was worried about. It was his friends and the crew on the Green Ship. Then there was Dagena. Where was she? He had caught a glimpse of her scurrying away into the darkness. He had not heard her voice, so she was still out there somewhere, cold and alone. The thought made him angry and desperate and, once again, he found himself struggling against his bonds, but it was no use. He tried to sit up but since his wrists were bound behind him to his ankles, he found it hard. He glanced around for a sharp object he might use to sever the ropes but he could see nothing in the darkness.

For what seemed like an eternity, he waited for something to happen, anything to relieve the boredom. Every now and then, he could hear the voice of Sir William or one of his men, and sometimes the wailing of the creature, or whatever it was that tormented the stillness of the night. He was about to call out in frustration when suddenly the tent flap opened. The scraggly bearded man, who had thrown him into the tent reached in and effortlessly scooped him up and carried him outside, where he was dropped near the fire next to Sir William, who was once again chewing on a piece of fish. Clement was lying on his back, looking up at him with disgust, as he licked the grease off his fingers.

"You are a traitor!"

Sir William shrugged and smiled condescendingly. "That depends."

"No! It is a fact! You have betrayed me and your king!"

"Oh yes, that much is true, but Henry is not my king. In fact, I do homage to no king," Sir

William said yawning, as if the subject were boring him. "Not even King Louis. But you might wonder why I have dragged you out here. I do believe there is someone here who might interest you."

He snapped his fingers and a tall looming shadow appeared from beyond the periphery of the campfire. At first, Clement thought that he might be dreaming, but when the man kneeled in front of him and smiled, showing a set of broken teeth under a crooked nose, he knew what he was seeing was real. The man was shaking his head and smiling devilishly and, for the first time in a long while, Clement found himself speechless.

"My stupid, arrogant nephew. I am the last person that you thought you would see out here in this wasteland, but here I am!"

Sven the Terrible stood up and swiftly kicked the boy in the ribs with the toe of his boot. Clement gasped for breath, but Sven was not yet done with his nephew. He kneeled again and, with his dagger, cut the rope that connected his wrists to his ankles and hauled him to his feet. Clement was grimacing as Sven held him firmly by the front of his cloak so that their faces were merely inches apart. He tried to look away from his uncle but when he did, he felt the back of Sven's large leathery hand slapping his cheek.

"Look at me!"

Clement did so, his eyes red and watery.

"Not so bold and brazen now, are you, nephew?"

"Your breath stinks!" Clement managed to say, anger and pride once again overcoming him.

Sven backhanded him again and dropped him down to the ground in front of the fire. Clement could taste blood. He expected another kick, or a sword to come slashing down on him, but neither came. Instead, Sven kneeled and sat his nephew up. Pulling off the boy's wool cap, he grabbed a hold of his long blond locks and pulled back. Clement winced, expecting to feel a blow from his powerful fist, but his uncle merely wagged his finger in front of his face.

"I arranged this whole thing. Don't you see it, nephew? When I found out about the Templar treasure and contacted Sir William..."

"What? The Templar treasure?" Clement asked. He was aghast.

Sven turned his head to the side and cocked an eyebrow at Sir William. The ugly scar on his face made Clement's wicked uncle seem even more intimidating.

"You are not as bright as I thought, nephew. Sir Humphrey Rochford does not sail for the king of France. He sails for Pope Alexander, but that does not matter. You are going to draw us a map in the morning and give it to Sir William. You will then have served your usefulness."

Clement was glaring at his uncle with hate.

"I have already given him a map."

Sven glanced at Sir William.

"Is this true?"

Sir William nodded.

"Yes, Sven. I thought I told you that."

Sven's red eyes narrowed. "You told me you could not get to Vinland without him. If you have a map, why do we need this little brat?"

Sir William was fidgeting nervously. He knew Sven's temper and did not wish to test it on this night.

"He...he is the only one who is skilled in the use of the astrolabe...and...and he also knows the stars and can plot a course."

For a few moments, there was silence. Sven glanced down at the boy, who had lowered his head.

"Are you not a navigator?" Sven asked, turning back to Sir William.

"Aye, but not like him."

Sven reached down and, once again, hauled Clement to his feet. He was smiling. A wicked grin of triumph realizing he had finally beat his nephew after suffering humiliating defeat in battle to the boy's rag tag army the previous year.

"I would like nothing more than to gouge your eyes out and let you wander this desolate landscape until you starve to death. But, due to Sir William's incompetence, it seems you have been given a stay of execution."

Clement thought about remaining silent, knowing the more he provoked his uncle the greater chance he would retaliate with abuse. But he could not help himself. It was not in his nature. He was Clement, son of Hugo, and, though still a boy, he would take no insult from any man. He did what his uncle least expected. He spit in his face. Sven's superior grin immediately evaporated and his brow seemed to split in two. He slowly reached up and wiped his face with the sleeve of his cloak.

"You are going to regret that," he said calmly. He whistled sharply and the scraggly bearded man, once again, appeared. Clement had already pegged this man as his personal jailor. He recognized him as one of the burly men-at-arms on Sir William's ship, but did not know his name.

"Lamberto, I want you to bring me one of this belligerent and disrespectful boy's fingers so that I can roast it over the fire and leave it as an offering to that savage monster that lurks out there in the darkness."

With that said, he kicked the back of Clement's knees, causing him to lose his balance and almost fall into the fire. He landed hard on his right shoulder.

Lamberto's eyes began to sparkle. He started to crack his knuckles in anticipation of his wickedness.

"Sire, the lad has defiled ye with his spittle. May I suggest a more appropriate punishment. I can remove his tongue if you so wish."

Sven seemed to consider this and he let Clement know it by hesitating to answer the jailor.

"Nay, we may need his tongue. A finger will do."

Lamberto bowed, pulled his dagger from his sheath, and moved toward the boy. Clement instinctively attempted to defend himself by kicking at the brute, but his ankles were still bound and the big man merely grabbed them.

"Take your filthy hands off me, you low born scoundrel!" Clement screamed.

Suddenly and unexpectedly, Sven interrupted the scene.

"No…no, not here, Lamberto. Take him into the tent and do it. I am a Christian man and if I were to witness something this savage, it might not play well with my sensibilities. Oh, and I don't want to hear his suffering, so you will need to stifle the little monster!"

Clement's uncle broke out into a fit of laughter, which Sir William did not find in the least amusing.

"Perhaps we are being a bit rash and hasty," Sir William said. "The boy might need all of his fingers to use the astrolabe."

Sven's smile disintegrated and he looked at Sir William coldly.

"He will have to get by with one less now, won't he?"

Lamberto lifted Clement over his shoulder like a sack of grain and carried the kicking and screaming boy into the tent, where he once again dumped him onto the cold earth, before departing for a brief interval and returning with an oil lamp and a cloth.

"You do not want to do this!" Clement screamed desperately.

"I am tired of ye disrespectful tongue, boy!"

Lamberto quickly tied the cloth around Clement's mouth and began sharpening his dagger on a stone. He was humming a tune and in no way seemed bothered by the boy's thrashing movements as his prisoner attempted to free himself. Then, with a devilish look of sadistic pleasure, he advanced toward the terrified boy with the sharpened blade. But... he never arrived at his destination. The iron skillet crashed against the jailer's head with a sickening thud and Lamberto landed face down, inches away from his now former prisoner.

Dagena stood over the prostrate form of the jailer, shaking her head.

"Well, that was rather easy," she said, twirling the skillet playfully in front of her. She quickly pulled the cloth away from Clement's mouth.

"Dagena! Thank God!"

She held a finger to her lips.

"Quiet, Clement, do you want the whole world to hear you," she whispered.

His face was beaming, "No, Dagena, only you, but, uh...can you untie me so we can get out of here?"

She freed him and when he stood up, he noticed that Lamberto was stirring slightly and starting to groan. Before his senses had returned, the skillet once again came crashing down on his head.

"That should keep him quiet until we are miles from here. He will have an egg on each side of his head, and no finger as a prize," she said with droll humor and began chuckling.

Clement joined her in the quiet, childish laughter, but then reality took hold of them. They still had to escape from this tent. At any moment, Sven or one of his cohorts might come dashing in, wondering what the delay was about and they needed to be long gone when it happened.

"Dagena, I need to get my bow," he said, barely above a whisper.

She had a playful smirk on her face.

"Don't you know me by now Clement. I have already taken care of that."

He gave her a sideways glance, smiled, and then picked up his former tormenter's dagger and stuffed it in his empty sheath. Grabbing her hand, he peaked out of the tent flap. Most of the men were lounging around a handful of fires. He could see Sven with his back toward him and, for a second, he thought of letting his dagger fly, but the thought was an emotional one and he knew it was irrational. His only thought now was for Dagena's safety.

"Come on, no one is looking," he said. They took off in a run and had soon scaled one of the small rocky hills, being extremely quiet and careful to avoid the pickets Sir William had placed on the periphery of the camp.

"Your bow and quiver are at the longhouse," Dagena said suddenly. "Along with some other items I thought we might need. I found a shortcut across the ridgeline."

"I sure do hope we do not encounter that monster tonight," Clement said wearily. "I have only this dagger to defend us with at the moment."

"Remember what Gorm told us," Dagena said. "Let us take his counsel and use it wisely."

"Aye, Dagena. Gorm is one of a kind, and a seer of the highest order. We are fortunate to have him. If we should encounter this beast, let us treat it not in the manner of the unfortunate Trousett."

After crossing the ridgeline, they soon found themselves at the top of a small rocky and windswept hillock. Clement recognized it from earlier except it was now pitch dark, with only the moonlight to light their way. As they were standing there looking down into the valley toward the longhouse, the sky suddenly began to shimmer in a glistening green light. Waves and ribbons of green and velvet danced across the heavens in majestic harmony with the stars.

"Oh, look Clement! It is beautiful!"

Mesmerized by the sight, the two youths stood there in awe, despite the cold and frigid air.

"Why, it is the Northern Lights," Clement said suddenly.

"I have never seen anything like it," she said.

He smiled. "Our ancestors say it is a skybridge from the earth to the heavens."

"Maybe it is beckoning us to follow! It is almost as if we have found paradise, Clement!" she said, turning to him.

He was holding both of her hands and no longer looking at the aerial phenomena that bathed them in the placid light of love. He was looking at her. He then brought her close to him and they kissed. For a moment or so, they just held each other, his arms wrapped around her waist and her hands caressing his long blond locks. The heavens danced.

Suddenly, she stopped kissing him. "Clement, where is your cap?"

Embarrassed, he placed his left hand on his head as if he were searching for it."

"Oh...yes, my wicked uncle is nothing like you, Dagena. He would rather pull my hair than play with it," he said with a chuckle.

She playfully imitated that act and they both started giggling.

"We had better grab my bow. By now, they have found out I have escaped. Once I have my bow, there is not a man alive who can hurt us, Dagena."

He grabbed her hand and they hurried down the wind-swept hill into the valley and were soon at the longhouse. Clement's bow and quiver were next to the old broken table they had found earlier that day. Dagena had also snatched a wool blanket, a water horn and some hard biscuits that she had stuffed in a pouch. She strapped it to her shoulders.

"Do you think they will come here looking for us?" she asked.

He was attaching his quiver to his belt and peering up at the ridgeline from which they had just come.

"I don't know, Dagena, but some of them know of this place so we cannot risk it. We must keep walking into the night."

"I heard some of them talking," she said. "They are afraid of that monster."

"Well, Sven won't be. He will come searching. He hates me, and when he finds out that I have eluded him again, his wrath will not be tamed by reason... and you, Dagena...you too will be one of his intended victims. I will not let that happen."

They continued onward, heading northwest, using Clement's knowledge of the stars to guide him. By his reckoning, they were hugging the coast of this strange land. He wanted to keep the sea in sight. There was a possibility his men might be able to take back the Green Ship, and, if he could possibly signal to them from the shore, there was a chance they might be rescued. Sir William had told him he had boarded his men on the Green Ship, but he wondered if it was a bluff. He could not picture in his mind, Jacques or

Baldwin surrendering, or being caught off guard. They would have been either tricked or fought to the death. Ultimately, the burden of responsibility fell on him. He was the admiral of this fleet and had, thus far, been outmaneuvered. However, he was not yet defeated.

They walked on in the darkness, holding hands and feeling a somewhat ethereal and almost supernatural strength from the shimmering green lights in the northern sky. They were careful with their footsteps, trying to avoid the snowy patches that would reveal their tracks to their possible pursuers. The undulating landscape was gravelly, with hardened moss and the occasional stand of willows. They must have traveled a few miles before Clement found what he was looking for. It was a rocky overhang on the side of a cliff. A perfect place to shelter for the rest of the night. The chances of Sven finding them here was so remote as to be almost non-existent. He could even start a small fire with some of the willow branches. He estimated they were at least three miles from the camp and the fire would be hidden from view by the cliff wall, even from the highest point on the ridge line.

He gathered some loose branches and some dead moss and began making a fire pit with some rocks. The temperature had dropped rapidly since they had escaped from the camp and he noticed Dagena shivering miserably, despite her warm wool cloak.

"Don't worry, Dagena. I will have a fire burning in no time. You will see," he said cheerily.

He went to work with his flint and steel while she sat with her back up against the rock, smiling and watching him. Every so often, he would glance at her and smile back. Finally, there was a spark and his cheeks went to work, blowing on the dead moss. He added a few twigs and soon had a small fire burning. He had dragged a dead willow back and began hacking away at the limbs with his sharp dagger.

"And to think this dagger almost hacked my finger off a short while ago," he said, turning to Dagena.

She shook her head. The smile had not left her face.

When he was done, he added enough fuel to keep the fire burning for at least an hour. He sat with his bow in his lap next to Dagena, who had thrown the blanket across their shoulders. For the first time since their escape from the camp, they heard the wailing sound of the lonely beast, but neither of them feared it.

"What do you think that creature is?" she asked him.

He was looking into the distance, thinking about her question, and finally turned to her.

"Tonight, it is our protector from evil. Are you warm enough, Dagena?"

She nodded.

"Yes, Clement. Are you?"

He shrugged.

"As long as you are here with me, Dagena."

They gazed up at the dancing heavens. The night was crystal clear and, suddenly, a shooting star blazed across the cold firmament, streaking across Orion's Belt. A short time later, the wind began to blow the powdered snow off the cliff above them, threatening to extinguish their warm fire, but neither one cared, for they had each other.

Chapter 15

It was still dark when Dagena woke. The fire was reduced to hot coals but she was still warm enough in her cloak under the blanket. She looked at Clement, who was still sleeping soundly. His bare, uncovered head resting on the cold rock troubled her and she removed her scarf and placed it beneath his head. He barely stirred. There was no question in her mind he would die for her. She would do the same. She would die for him. Quietly she rose, being careful not to wake him. The fiery starlit heavens had vanished and had succumbed to a cloudy dark sky that seemed ominous for the day ahead of them. She blew on the hot coals and a flame appeared. It was not long before she had a fire blazing again. Clement had dragged enough willow branches to their camp to last a few more hours. She was glad she had thought to grab the biscuits. It was not much, but it would relieve the gnawing hunger for at least a few days.

"Dagena, you should have woken me," Clement said with a yawn. He sat up and was stretching his arms over his head.

She added a stick to the flames.

"It will be light soon," she said, kneeling next to the fire.

"We have to get to the shore and look for the Green Ship. It is our only chance off this place," he said quietly.

She was preparing a few of the biscuits for their morning meal by warming them over the open flames.

"The Green Ship...yes, Clement, but what if Sven and Sir William have taken it over. Then what?"

He was biting his lip and lowered his head.

"I do not know, Dagena. I guess our only option would be to remain here. What choice would we have? We cannot swim home."

She looked at him with a serious expression but then burst out laughing. The laughter was contagious.

"What? What did I say?" he asked with a wide grin.

"I think we can swim, Clement; it is only a few thousand miles."

He stood up, hitched his quiver back on his belt, and slung the bow over his shoulder.

"It is getting lighter. I am going to take a walk up on that ridge and see if I can see anything."

"Oh no, you are not," she said. "You are going to eat something first and then we will break down this camp and go together. There is no way I am going to sit here by myself in this God forsaken place."

He shrugged.

"You are right Dagena. What was I thinking? I guess I am just anxious to explore, that is all."

He sat down next to her and she passed him a biscuit. He took a few nibbles and, surprisingly, found he was not that hungry.

"How many of these biscuits did you grab?" he asked, looking at the bulging leather pouch.

"All of them. About fifteen or so. Alice and Osment baked them over the fire pit yesterday, so they should last us a few days. It is fortunate we brought supplies to the shore."

Clement was pressing his thumbs into his biscuit.

"Well, I like being prepared for everything, but I honestly must say that I did not expect to see Sir William and should have anticipated his treachery, especially after King Henry's warning. Although, I am still puzzled by why King Henry let him come along when he was aware he might be working for King Louis."

"Well, I am not," Dagena said angrily. "I think King Henry was using both of you. He wants whatever is in that chest and he wants it bad enough to play people like pieces on a chess board."

Clement was still pressing his thumbs into the biscuit and seemed to be immersed in deep thought.

"Are you going to eat that biscuit or play with it?" Dagena asked, as if she were addressing a small child instead of a teenager.

"Oh...sorry. I was just thinking, that is all."

"About what?"

He took a bite of the biscuit and began chewing it mechanically.

"About what Sven said. He mentioned the Templar treasure and Sir William told me that he was working for King Louis. Now neither of those scoundrels are working for anyone other than themselves. I know that now. King Henry told me he was not sure who this Sir Humphrey Rochford was, but that he believed he was sailing for King Louis. I do not believe that. I believe both kings are working together to steal the treasure from the Templar fleet."

She looked puzzled.

"Then why did King Henry need you?"

"He knew I was the only one, besides the Templars, with the navigational skills to find Vinland."

"And one more question. Why did King Henry tell you Sir William was a spy? And why did Sir William not let you lead them to Vinland before usurping your command?"

He swallowed the rest of his biscuit.

"That is two questions, Dagena," he said with a smirk, holding up two fingers. She playfully tapped him on the head with her thumb and he laughed.

"King Henry probably hoped I would arrest Sir William and then he would not have to share whatever is in the chest with King Louis. It is the only explanation I can think of. I failed to do that, and Sir William would have let me lead him all the way to Vinland and back, had it not been for his chance encounter with my uncle Sven, who has been wanting his revenge on me for the past year now. Remember the day Adam and I were attacked by those two ruffians in Harfleur?"

"Yes, why?"

Clement was tightening the lace on one of his boots.

"Well, Sir William claims he dispatched one of those rogues after we left him bloodied in the road. Sir William did no such thing. Sven was in town that day and Sir William sent him a message. The two men then hatched a diabolical scheme to rid themselves of me, but at the same time use me as a means to capture the Templar treasure."

Dagena had folded her hands in front of her and had thrown her head back so it was resting on the slab of rock.

"That sounds like a valid theory, Clement," she said. "But how do they think they are going to take this treasure from the Templars? They are not just going to hand it over to them. Also, why follow them all the way to Vinland? Why not just attack them and steal the treasure before the fleet left Normandy?"

"I don't know, Dagena, but greed is a funny thing. I suspect they did not want to blatantly attack the Templar's fleet with witnesses who would draw the ire of Pope Alexander. They would be excommunicated and who knows what else. Also, perhaps they believe the treasure is already in Vinland."

He picked up a pebble and threw it into Dagena's lap. She looked at it and then noticed him smiling at her.

"For someone whose fortunes have fallen you are in a cheery mood," she said, throwing the pebble back at him.

"Well, I have a lot to be cheerful about," he responded.

She rolled her eyes. "Oh sure, here we are being chased by sea pirates, in a land barren of just about everything, with no means of escape, and some sort of monster lurking out there in the darkness that tears people apart, just waiting to do the same to us. What's there not to be cheerful about?"

He leaned forward and added a few sticks to the flames.

"Dagena, it could be worse. I could be all alone and so could you."

She was rolling another pebble between her cold fingers and flung it at him.

"You're right, Clement. We have each other, don't we?"

He nodded and stared off into the cold abyss. For the first time in a few hours, they heard the wailing of the beast.

"I think we had better get moving, Dagena,"

Closing their camp, they moved on. Clement wanted to get a good look at the surrounding country; so, they climbed to the top of the cliff, being careful to watch their footing on the icy and snow-covered rocks. The wind was blowing hard and he wished he had his wool cap, but he was fortunate to have the hood of his cloak which somewhat buffered the cold breeze. It was now light enough to be able to see for a few miles in every direction and he was elated to see the Green Ship still sitting in the bay, south of them. It appeared like a small speck, but it was there. The Red Ship had moved abreast of his vessel, but the Brown Ship was anchored further up the bay. To the southeast, Sven's camp was blocked by the ridge, but he could see the valley and the longhouse and the sparse forest of willows.

"Clement, look!"

She was pointing toward the longhouse.

"I think there are people there. Something is moving."

He pulled his small glass from his cloak pocket and aimed it. He could see the unmistakable forms of nearly a dozen men searching the area around the longhouse.

"We were right not to stay there," he said, swallowing nervously.

She took the glass from him and peered through it, returning it to him with a shudder.

"They won't stop looking until they find us," she said. "You are the only one who has the navigational skills to get them to Vinland."

He put the glass back in his cloak and pointed toward the Green Ship.

"Dagena, there sits the Green Ship, anchored and waiting for us. It is our only chance. We need to get closer to determine if we can tell if my men have control of it. If Sven's men have taken it, we are trapped."

They walked along the ridgeline for a while and found the climb down to the beach rather grueling. In some areas it was covered with ice and, on more than one occasion, they slipped. When they reached the bottom, they started walking south toward the bay and found, to their dismay, it was a longer walk than they had anticipated.

"Oh, my feet are getting sore," Dagena complained. "This gravel is rather bothersome."

"We do not have much further to go and then I want to climb up onto those rocks and have a look. We do not want to get too close."

They continued onward until they neared a bend. A towering cliff blocked their view of the bay.

"When we turn this corner, we will be able to see the ships," he said. "Let us find a good place to observe them."

Climbing up a hill, they had to walk inland a little before turning back and finding a route which led them through a maze of boulders and a twisted landscape, devoid of any life. Suddenly, the bay came into view and the Green Ship appeared once again, this time so close they could see men working on the deck. The first thing Clement realized was he had indeed lost his ship. The men working the deck were not his own. He recognized a few of them from Sir William's crew.

"It's Jacques!" Dagena exclaimed loudly, looking through the glass.

Clement saw him at almost the same time. He appeared to be chained to the mast and was watching his captors closely, undoubtedly looking for an opportunity.

"Well, at least they are alive," Clement said. "I wonder where the others are?"

"I don't know," she said. "But they must have made it back. There sits the boat on the deck."

For a while, they just sat there among the rocks, in desperate silence. The troubling scene below them appearing like a bad dream.

"If there was only a way to get on that ship," Clement said finally.

"And then what?" Dagena asked. "Become a captive like Jacques and the others? That is foolish thinking, Clement."

She was watching his reaction and he suddenly grinned.

"Oh, no! I don't like the look of this!" she said. "What are you thinking?"

"I have a plan," he said, showing her his teeth and holding up a finger.

"You always have a plan, Clement. Let me hear it, and I will tell you if it is feasible, or if you are mad in the head."

He sat back against the boulder and folded his arms over his knees. He was still smiling.

"Dagena, it might sound crazy, but the first thing we need to do is alert them. I estimate the Green Ship is about a hundred yards away, as the crow flies. I am going to wait until the deck is clear of everyone except Jacques and then I am going to launch an arrow above his head, into the mast. He will know it is me. All my arrows are marked with my initials, as you well know, Dagena."

She was rubbing her round chin and shaking her head. A dubious expression lighting up her cold face.

"You might hit Jacques. The wind is blowing rather hard, Clement."

He was already inspecting one of his arrows.

"The wind is blowing off the cliff to the south. This will help the arrow in its flight, and I will not hit Jacques. I promise, Dagena."

"What will this prove, Clement?"

"They will know we have escaped. That is what this will prove."

He armed his bow. His eyes carefully scanned the deck of the ship, waiting for his chance. Jacques was seated against the mast and there were only two men besides him on the deck. One of them was carrying a bucket and soon disappeared below deck. The other man was standing at the rail, drinking from a horn but was facing him. When he turned and started walking toward the sterncastle, Clement let the arrow fly. He saw Jacques jerk his head upwards and then, with a look of astonishment, glanced in the direction from which the arrow had come. Clement stood up, gesticulating wildly, and, when he was certain that Jacques had seen him, he slid back down next to Dagena, who had closed her eyes.

"I did not want to look," she said, opening them.

"What is the matter, Dagena? Don't you trust me by now?" he said with a proud smile.

"Now what?"

"This evening we will take the smallest boat and row it aside of the Green Ship," he said with a nod.

"And how will we manage that, Clement? Are we going to just walk into Sven's camp, and ask him if we can use the boat? And even if we do somehow manage to get it to the Green Ship, how will we get on board without help?"

"I think I am scrawny enough to fit through one of the oarlock ports, but I will have to get it open somehow as it is latched from the inside. That will be a trick, Dagena...but let me think about it for a while. I am sure I can come up with something."

Her mouth dropped. She leaned forward and placed her hands on his cheeks.

"Clement, let me understand you. We are going to steal a boat, row up the fjord in the dark, somehow get the boat up alongside the Green Ship and then you are going to climb through an oarlock port, after which you will encounter at least a dozen of Sven's men, who will be below deck. Then you will free Jacques and the others and we will then sail off into the sunset?"

He winked. "Yea, something like that, but Sven's men will be dead drunk. I will walk all over them and they won't even stir."

She let go of his cheeks and pulled his ear.

"That is the craziest thing that I ever heard, Clement...but...it might just work!"

He became excited and grabbed her hands.

"See, Dagena, we think alike!"

"Maybe," she said, "but what will we do now?"

He sat there thinking, wrinkling his nose and playing with the lace on one of his boots.

"We need to find a place to hide near Sven's camp, where we can watch and wait until all his men are drunk and asleep tonight. Then we can steal our way into the camp and grab the small boat."

Dagena was thinking about her sore feet.

"That is going to be a long walk the way we came. Clement. Perhaps we can cut the distance somehow."

"Yes," Clement said. "And there is the small forest with all those willows and birch trees we saw from the slope earlier. We could explore it. I doubt that Sven will look for us there."

They started off, climbing back through the maze of boulders. They finally reached the top of the ridge and followed it down until it leveled off into the valley, where they entered the forest. The trees here were taller than any others they had seen in this land and there was a babbling stream that curved around the mossy rocks like a serpent.

"Dagena, look!"

Growing out of a fissure in the rocks was a plant with dark blue berries. They soon noticed hundreds of them growing along the banks of the stream.

"Do you think they are edible?" Dagena asked.

Clement plucked one, popped it in his mouth, and chewed it. He made a gurgling noise and grabbed his throat in mock amusement, as if it might be poisonous. Dagena turned white as a sheet before she noticed the boy laughing hysterically at his own humor.

"Clement! That was not funny!"

He suddenly felt terrible when he noticed tears in her eyes.

"Oh! Oh! Dagena. How stupid of me!"

He hugged her.

"I...I don't think sometimes, Dagena."

"No, you don't," she said, pulling away from him angrily. "Let us fill this pouch with some of these berries. We can have them with our biscuits later."

"And maybe I can catch a few fish!" he added, hoping to boost her spirits.

She ignored him and they went to work filling the pouch. They followed the stream, frozen over in spots until it disappeared into a large network of boulders. Finally, they started up another ridge, close to the old Norse longhouse. They were careful to scan the area around them as they were nearing Sven's camp. Scrambling halfway down the hill, they found a good spot to observe the camp. It was just as they had left it, except for one thing. The boats were missing.

"Where is everyone?" Dagena asked skeptically. "You would think they would have left a guard while they were out looking for us."

"I don't know. Dagena, but the boats are gone!"

She looked at him with a look of horror.

"Do you think they gave up looking for us and left?"

He was silent, pensive, his eyes searching the camp for clues, but Dagena was full of questions.

"Why would they just leave the tents and supplies?"

He was shaking his head when, suddenly, the reality of their situation hit him.

"The Green Ship!"

Grabbing Dagena by the hand, they scrambled around the backside of the camp and trekked along the shoreline. They followed it until they reached the point where the fjord opened into the bay. From here, they had a bird's eye view of the surrounding region. Holding hands and standing on the highest point they gazed out at the bay. In the distance three sails could be seen moving in tandem, as if they were linked together by a chain.

"They...they have abandoned us," Dagena said.

Clement felt a sickening knot tighten in his stomach and he felt Dagena's hand tighten. They looked at each other in silence. For a while, they merely stood there watching the sails, until they finally disappeared on the southwestern horizon. By that time, it was getting close to dusk and they decided there was nothing left to do except go back to the camp and see what was left behind. By the time they arrived, it was almost dark and Clement immediately set to work building a fire, while Dagena took inventory of their stock.

"They left in a hurry, Clement. Osment's medical chest is still here and they did not take any of the smoked meat and wheat."

"Well, at least we won't go hungry, Dagena. I am surprised Sven did not destroy it before he left, just to spite us."

Dagena had explored the largest tent and was about to enter the second one, when she saw something that took her breath away.

"Oh my God, Clement, look!"

She was pointing to the hard-packed snow that gradually receded down toward the shore, where the boats had been. A series of large footprints were intermingled with the boot prints from the men. They followed them and discovered traces of blood on the rocks. Around the bend they found the first body, and then another, and finally a third, which looked vaguely familiar to them. It was on its side and when Clement turned the twisted and distorted corpse over onto its back, the left arm did not come with it. It was detached and resting in a pool of coagulated blood.

"We know now why they left in a hurry," Clement said, peering down at the battered lifeless face of Sir William de Bayeux.

They walked slowly back to the camp, carefully listening to the sounds of the night. It was quiet, Clement thought, almost too quiet. They sat together in front of the fire, nibbling on the biscuits and berries, aware that whatever it was that killed those men was out there lurking and waiting, perhaps even now stalking the camp, watching them.

"Maybe, just maybe, those men attacked it," Dagena said hopefully. "We will not do that, Clement. We will be its friends."

Clement shrugged. "It is some sort of animal, Dagena. I do not know if it has the capability of reason, but perhaps...like a dog. A dog will attack an intruder but obey its master. But this creature is feral...I do not know, Dagena, but we will take Gorm's advice. We do not have much of a choice."

Dagena was about to respond when, suddenly, she perceived movement behind one of the tents. She attempted to warn Clement but found herself rendered speechless by fear. She pointed, her finger shaking. He reacted quickly. Pulling Dagena to her feet, he immediately pushed her behind him and, dagger held in front of him, he stood between her and the large silhouette looming in the darkness. The shadow advanced into the glow of the campfire and took the form of a man, sword in hand. The man let out a loud bellowing laugh that echoed through the cold night. Lamberto raised the sword, a troubled look of insanity permeating his entire being as he moved toward them.

Chapter 16

Clement slowly backed up, holding his dagger tightly in front of him and pushing Dagena backwards at the same time.

Lamberto seemed confused and in the light of the fire, Clement could see why. His former jailer's mouth was partly open and the lips were swollen into a grotesque shape that deformed the lower part of his face, but it was not the cause of the big man's confusion. It was the eyes. They were missing! Only two bloodied, empty sockets remained. They had been gouged out by something and then Clement remembered Sven threatening to gouge his own eyes out. It was obvious; Lamberto had become the victim of Sven's wrath. This was his punishment for letting Clement escape.

"He is blind, Dagena! He cannot hurt us!"

Lamberto had slowly eased himself up to the fire, feeling its warmth. He lowered his sword and waved it out in front of him, as if he were using it as a guide to lead him. His head turned toward the direction of Clement's voice but he did not proceed any further. He merely stood there, looking lost and stupid. His face was caked with blood and Dagena wondered how he was still standing.

"Sit!" Clement ordered, as if he were talking to a dog instead of a man.

For a few seconds, the brute just stood there, his head tilted toward the direction of the boy's voice. He mumbled something, but it was incoherent. His lips moved in rapid succession. Finally, he shoved the blade of his sword in the earth at his feet and, gripping the hilt, he lowered himself down, sitting cross legged in front of the fire.

"You...you are a wicked man and I should plunge this dagger through your heart," Clement said sternly. "Now take that sword and throw it off to the side of you!"

The brute cocked his head and feeling for the hilt of his weapon, he grasped it and reluctantly performed the task. He was completely at their mercy and he knew it. He attempted to speak again but only a series of garbled utterances issued forth from his bloodied mouth. When he opened it wide, Clement could see with horror why. They had cut out his tongue.

"My God, Dagena. The savagery! They have cut half his tongue out!"

The disfigured brute moved his head and began to laugh, the same painful guttural laugh they had heard before. The man had obviously gone mad. Clement wondered why he did not drive the sword through himself to end his torment but realized the will and instinct to live and survive was ingrained in most people, despite their hardships.

"Lamberto? That is your name, right?" Clement asked.

He nodded and mumbled something that sounded like, "aye."

"I have no pity for you but we are not savages, like my uncle who did this to you, despite the way you ill-treated me. Do you understand?"

He grunted and shook his head in the affirmative. Dagena began to feel bad for him. Clement started to move closer to him, but Dagena grabbed his arm.

"He's still dangerous, Clement. He is twice your size and strength. If he grabs hold of you..."

Clement stopped and the brute began shaking his head and moaning as if he might be attempting to say, "no."

"Lamberto, I am going to ask you some questions and you are going to either nod your head or shake it. Do you understand?" Clement asked.

Lamberto nodded and grunted in the affirmative. His swollen lips and crushed nose reminded Clement of a head of cabbage.

"Did Sven kill my men?"

He shrugged and then shook his head.

"Does that mean you do not know?"

He nodded.

"Will you try to hurt me or Dagena if we let you live?"

He shook his head and a slight guttural laugh emanated from the back of his throat, but Clement was not sure if it was one of irony related to his new situation, or one meant to be evil. Dagena had not removed her eyes from him, still clinging nervously on Clement's arm.

"Do you trust him?" Dagena whispered in Clement's ear.

He shook his head. "No, but what can he do? Without us, he is as good as dead and he knows it."

"But he is insane. I can feel it," she responded.

"Maybe, but what do we do?"

Lamberto edged forward, attempting to hear what the two youths were whispering to one another.

"Well, I won't trust staying in this camp with him. Even if he is lame and disfigured," she said.

"I agree, but we do not have to murder him," he whispered. "Maybe we can lead him out of the camp for the night, while we are sleeping, and give him a blanket so he will not freeze to death. There will be no way he could find his way back here in the darkness to hurt us."

She nodded. "But how?"

"Leave that to me."

He turned back to Lamberto, who was still straining to hear the conversation. He knew that it revolved around him.

"Lamberto!" he said in a stern voice. "This is what we are going to do. We are going to give you a blanket and lead you away from the camp. At daylight, we will lead you to another place and give you food and water. Do you understand?"

He grunted and made another guttural sound as if he understood.

"Get a blanket and some rope, Dagena."

She hurried into the big tent, returned with the blanket, and handed the rope to Clement. He tied the rope in a slip knot loop. Being careful not to get too close to the big man, he used it as a lasso and threw it over the brute's shoulders and pulled. Lamberto grunted like an animal.

"Sorry, Lamberto, but it is the only way," Clement said, "At least you don't have to worry about me cutting your finger off, though I probably should for the way you treated me."

He yanked on the rope and Lamberto stood up. Clement slung his bow over his shoulder and Dagena followed with the blanket. They walked slowly into the darkness, guided only by the moonlight and the stars. Every now and then, Clement tugged on the rope as the big man slowly ambled along. Finally, they came to the ridge that overlooked the valley with the longhouse. Clement estimated they were at least a half a mile from their camp. A blind man could not possibly find his way back.

"We stop here," Clement said.

Lamberto stopped and turned slightly to his left, as if he were attempting to ascertain where Clement might be. He once again attempted to speak but only succeeded in forcing a trickle of blood to roll down his chin. Clement attempted to loosen the rope around Lamberto by wiggling it back and forth, but this only caused it to tighten.

"Lamberto, use your hands and pull the rope apart," Clement said impatiently. He was tired and wanted to get back to the camp. For a few seconds, the big man just stood there as if he had not heard the boy. Then with one quick jerk, Lamberto yanked on the rope and because Clement was still holding onto it, he came with it, losing his balance and falling at Lamberto's feet. The big man took advantage of the situation and scooped the boy up, pulling back on his neck. Dagena screamed and began beating the man with the sides of her fists but he merely pushed her to the ground with his free arm. Struggling, Clement managed to pull his dagger from his sheath and stab Lamberto in his calf, which caused the brute to immediately let go of the boy, who scrambled away on his hands and knees toward Dagena, who was pulling herself off the ground. What happened next was so unexpected and so sudden both of them could not believe what they were witnessing. A massive pale shadow rushed in from the darkness toward Lamberto, who was crawling toward where he thought Clement might be. Stopping for a few seconds, the monster hovered over Clement's attacker and then, stooping over, it picked the struggling man up over its head. Lamberto began making gurgling sounds as he found himself choking on his own blood. For another few seconds, the creature stood there and then, without warning, it slammed Lamberto down onto the rocks with such force that his neck immediately snapped. Clement and Dagena were clinging to one another, still on their knees, frozen in fear, looking up at the massive form of the creature, who now turned toward them. It was nearly ten feet tall, covered in white bristly hair with a large head and bulging black eyes that protruded from their sockets like pieces of coal. The mouth was wide and grotesque and, when it opened it, they could see the razor-sharp teeth as large as a man's fingers. For a while, it merely stood there glaring at them, surreal in the moonlight. Finally, it began to advance toward them. Clement did not even bother to attempt holding his dagger or bow against it. He remembered Gorm's words and he planned to adhere to them, though it might cost them their lives.

Finally, the creature stopped, hovering over them like a lion over its prey, but instead of crushing the life out of them, it did something else, something quite extraordinary. It squatted in front of them and gently touched them both on their heads with its huge leathery hand. It then stood up and turned away. With a few giant leaps and bounds, it sped off into the starry night, the wailing sound of its voice penetrating the lonely darkness.

They watched until it disappeared over the ridge. For a few minutes, they merely sat there, still trembling at the thought of the impossible thing they had just witnessed. It was Dagena who finally broke the silence.

"C...Clement?" she said.

He looked at her. He was biting his lower lip.

"Yea," he responded, barely above a whisper.

"Let's go home."

He nodded and, together, they stood up and gathered their things, both quickly glancing at the broken corpse of Lamberto. When they arrived back at the camp, the fire had burned down to coals, but they were in no mood to sit around a fire. They crawled into the biggest tent and made a comfortable and warm bed out of the wool blankets, which had, fortunately, been left behind. Neither one of them said a word. They were exhausted and quickly fell asleep, Clement cradling Dagena in his arms.

It was daylight when Clement finally opened his eyes. He sat up, wrapped in one of the warm wool blankets. Dagena was still sound asleep. He could see her red hair sticking out of the blankets but did not wish to disturb her. He quickly laced up his boots, stood up and stretched. He felt well refreshed and realized there was something about this morning that was different. It was now just him and Dagena. The Green Ship was gone. Everybody was gone. They were all alone, except for the monster, but this threat to their survival had vanished. The beast could have killed them both if it had chosen to do so. He felt the morning chill and decided a rip-roaring fire and some chicory water would do them good. They still had plenty of wood and he now knew where he could get more. He soon had a blaze going and the smell of smoke woke Dagena. Throwing a blanket over her cloak she walked outside. Clement was kneeling, breaking off limbs from a branch. She picked up a pebble and tossed it at him, hitting him in the back. He turned and smiled.

"How long did we sleep? The sun has been out a while," she said.

"I don't know, Dagena, but something feels different today."

She looked puzzled. "What do you mean?"

"I...I don't know really," he said, standing up. "I just feel different, that's all. It is hard to explain."

"Try," she retorted, sitting down in front of the flames. He sat next to her.

"I feel older or something. That's all."

She was looking at him curiously. "Is it because we kissed the other night?" She lowered her head and began chuckling, which caused him to follow along with her.

"Maybe, but we have kissed before, Dagena."

"But not like that!" she started giggling again.

He stared at her for a few seconds, a placid smile on his face, watching her brush her hair back. Her oval face was beaming.

"You…you did want me to kiss you like that?" he asked nervously.

"Of course, I did, Clement,"

She looked at him quickly and blushed. He looked up at the sky and pointed to a cloud.

"Let's play the cloud game, Dagena!"

Her face brightened as she stood.

"That is a great idea, Clement! Let us eat something first and then we can take a walk up on the ridge and we will be able to see the whole sky! We can pretend to be back in Normandy!"

They devoured a hearty breakfast of biscuits, with berries and a slab of smoked meat. Clement thought about trying to catch some fish. They had brought a net but the water was so cold he decided to put it off for another day. They still had plenty of food to last the two of them for at least a month or more. After that, they would be forced to hunt and fish out of necessity.

The days passed by swiftly and, for the most part, it was much of the same. Dagena would tend to the camp, while Clement went out to hunt, sometimes snagging a hare or a ptarmigan. Occasionally, she would go with him and they would sit on the top of the ridge, looking out at the ocean, often playing the cloud game or watching the seabirds in their flight. At night, they would sometimes hear the wailing of the beast. Clement had started calling it the snowman because of its white hair. Occasionally, they would see it from afar, but it never bothered them. They would sometimes go to the spot where Lamberto had attempted to kill them and leave an offering of fish, which the snowman gladly received.

It was nearly three weeks after they had watched the Green Ship sail away. Clement arose at dawn and decided it would be a good day for him and Dagena to take a hike up to the top of the ridge and watch the birds. It was a sunny morning with not a cloud in the sky. Dagena packed a couple of biscuits and some berries. They started off, reaching the summit after about half an hour. Clement carried his bow. He felt naked without it, even though he was certain he would not need it. They sat down on their favorite rock and looked out at the wide expanse of ocean. Sometimes, they would longingly look toward the western horizon, hoping to see the Green Ship but it never appeared and they had now almost given up hope of ever seeing it again, or, for that matter, ever seeing anything else except this barren wasteland.

It was Dagena who saw it first.

"Clement…what is that?"

"What?"

He had been daydreaming, thinking to himself how lucky he was to have Dagena here with him. She grabbed him by the shoulder and pointed toward the eastern horizon.

"That! What is it?"

Clement tried to focus his gaze on the general direction Dagena was pointing. He finally saw it, a small dark speck.

"I…I don't know. Is it an iceberg maybe?"

"Where is your glass?" she asked excitedly.

He felt for it in his cloak and pulled it out. He stood up and held it to his eye, squinting in the morning sunlight.

"It is a sail, Dagena!"

"What? Are you sure?"

She grabbed it from him and peered through it. The top of a ship's mast was plainly visible.

"The Green Ship!" she screamed.

He took the glass from her and looked through it again.

"Not from that direction, Dagena. The Green Ship sailed west; we would see it coming back from the west."

"But it might be, Clement!" she said hopefully. "What if it got thrown asunder in a storm?"

"No, Dagena, this is someone else. I am sure of it."

He continued to hold the glass to his eye. After a few more minutes, another speck appeared and then, almost at the same time, another. He swallowed hard.

"More sails, Dagena. It is certainly not the Green Ship. There is a distinct marking on the sail of the lead vessel but I cannot make it out. Friend or foe, I know not, but let us get back to the camp and hide some of our equipment in case they are an enemy."

"But who could they be? Certainly, they would not harm us."

Clement lowered the glass and placed a hand on her shoulder.

"There are a lot of Sven's in this world, Dagena. Let us hope this is not one of them. I am not going to put your life at risk. We need to be prepared for anything."

They returned to the camp and packed up some essentials, including blankets and food and placed it on one of the rolling carts. They dragged it nearly a mile inland, where they found a secluded spot in the rocks near where they found the berries. They returned to the ridge and, when they arrived at the top, they were astonished at the sight.

"My God, Dagena, look!"

A dozen ships of various sizes were entering the bay. The largest one compared in size with the Green Ship, with a large sterncastle and a smaller one on the bow. But it was the marking on the sail that told the story. A bright red cross.

"It's the Templar fleet, Dagena! We are saved!"

She grabbed him around the neck and kissed him, but then suddenly became sad.

"But, Clement…I…I was beginning to like this place."

He smiled. "Me too, Dagena."

They turned back toward the ships and it was not long before they had all entered the bay. Clement could see men on the deck, dressed in the white surcoats of the Templar order. They were all the same, emblazoned with the red cross over the chest. Most of them wore thick beards, but Clement noticed a small boy among them dressed in black, who emerged from the sterncastle with a man similarly attired. He was of average build, dressed in a black tunic and mantle with the red cross.

"He must be the leader!" Clement exclaimed with excitement. "I wonder if that is Sir Humphrey Rochford? It has to be!"

Dagena was perplexed.

"Clement, I thought the fleet of Sir Humphrey had left the port at Bretagne weeks before we left... and we were delayed in Ireland. They should be at least a month ahead of us, don't you think?"

Clement shook his head. "I don't know, Dagena, but this is the Templar fleet. They must have been delayed somehow."

They watched them lower the boats, about a dozen of them from at least half of the ships. Men in white coats and mantles, armed with swords began making their way toward the shore, but it was the largest boat, which held Clement's interest. A large skiff, holding a dozen men with a raised seat on the stern. It was here where the man in black sat, next to the boy. Clement thought the lad looked remarkably familiar. He aimed the glass toward the front of the boat, where a monk in a black robe sat in silent repose holding a large sturdy wooden cross, painted red. The boat moved slowly through the choppy water, bobbing up and down with the surf, the waves lapping at the sides. Clement fixed the glass back at the rear of the boat.

"That boy! I know him! It is Tristan!" Clement exclaimed suddenly. His mouth dropped. He fixed the glass back on the man sitting next to him. This man was undisputedly the leader of this fleet. He exuded strength and power. A warrior, who demanded respect and got it. The head was lowered, and when he lifted it, Clement thought he might be dreaming, but no... it was real! He could feel his heart racing. He closed his eyes and opened them but the man with the yellow beard and square jaw was still there. He now knew the rest of the story. Sir Humphrey Rochford did not exist, or at least not as King Henry or anyone else imagined it. Clement could hear the seagulls and waited. Adalbert de Langton had arrived.

End of Book 2

Glossary

Antechamber - A small room adjacent to a larger room.

Astrolabe - Instrument used for measuring the height and latitude of stars and planets.

Cog - A type of medieval sailing vessel. Typically using only one mast and sail

Chinon Castle - Residence of King Henry II. Located on the banks of the Vienne river in France.

Crenel - Open space on a castle flanked by Merlons. Used by archers.

Cresset - A metal pot containing a flammable substance, such as wood, oil or coal. Usually mounted on a pole

Galley - A type of ship that is manned by oars.

Hibernia - The Latin name for Ireland.

Knarr - A single mast cargo ship with a deep hull.

Kraken - A legendary sea monster of gigantic size. Sightings of this squid-like creature have been reported by mariners since ancient times, but mostly off the coasts of Greenland and Norway in the North Atlantic.

Máel Dúin - Legendary Irish explorer of the late 1st Millenium. He was said to have visited many islands and encountered various strange creatures and places.

Merlon - Upright, vertical section on a castle's wall or turret used for defense.

Picket - A sentry or guard that defends a camp. Mostly used to deliver an advance warning in case of attack.

Pintle-and-Gudgeon - A sophisticated type of rudder used to steer a ship.

Quay - A landing near the water used to load and offload goods from ships.

Sterncastle - (Stern Castle) Enclosed cabin on the stern of a ship.

Knights Templar - A Catholic military order founded in the early 12th century.

Tween Deck - Space between the deck and the cargo hold. It is usually used for storage.

Cast of Characters

Main Characters

Clement - 14-year-old Count of la Haye. Son of Hugo. Extremely intelligent. Fluent in a dozen languages. Expert archer and navigator.

Dagena - 14-year-old girlfriend of Clement. A former kitchen servant to Adalbert de Langton. Witty, smart and strong willed.

Olaf - 15-year-old loyal friend and right-hand man of Clement. Son of a Danish fisherman.

Supporting Characters

Alice - Daughter of Lord Mowbray. 14-year-old girlfriend of Olaf. Intelligent and adventurous

Osment - Son of Lord Tancerville. 14-year-old doctor of medicine.

Sven the Terrible - Clement's uncle. Evil, jealous and cruel. He chases after Clement with a vengeance.

Adam - 17-year-old woodcutter. Large and strong. Mentally challenged but brave and a good friend to Clement.

Agnes the Widow - Adam's mother.

Wedem - Ethiopian prince in exile. He was Count Hugo's best friend and a father figure to Clement.

Jacques the Giant - Clement's bodyguard and protector. He stands nearly 7 feet tall and weighs nearly 400 pounds.

William de Bayeux - Captain of the Brown Ship.

Roger de Montfort - Captain of the Black Ship.

Ceres the Greek - Captain of the Red Ship.

Mac Lochlainn - High king of the Irish.

Padraig O'Kane - Head of the Clan O'Kane and Dunseverick castle.

Tieg O'Kane- Son of Padraig O'Kane. Fights Clement and later becomes his friend.

Claude of York - Expert archer. Former acquaintance of Count Hugo.

O'Sullivan - Rector of Cork. An expert archer.

Rory - One of Padraig O'Kane's bodyguards.

Gorm - Old Danish sailor, friend of Clement and Dagena. He is also a storyteller.

Esteban - Skilled archer, loyal friend of Clement.

King Henry II - King of England (1154-1189)

Bernard - One of King Henry's servants.

Trousett - Cartographer and agent of King Henry.

Eustace - One of Clement's servants at la Haye castle.

Pierre - Clement's captain and loyal friend.

Marcel - A loyal knight. One of Clement's skilled swordsman.

Milton - A traveling minstrel. Friend of Clement and Dagena.

Countess de la Haye - Clement's great-aunt. Lives in Harfleur on the Norman coast.

Willem - Servant to the countess de la Haye.

Baldwin - Carpenter and skilled navigator of the Green Ship.

Bran - Baldwin's dog. A huge mastiff.

Drago - One of Clement's men-at-arms.

Lamberto - One of Sven the Terrible's evil henchmen.

Adalbert de Langton - Son of the Templar Knight, Robert de Langton. Seneschal of the Knights Templar and friend to Clement and Dagena.

Tristan - Adopted son of Adalbert de Langton. Saved by Robert de Langton from the Cathar village outside of Paris. (See the novel, Adalbert)

Count Hugo - Father of Clement. Murdered by one of Marcoul's henchmen. (See the novel, Adalbert)

About this Book

Clement: The Green Ship is book # 2 in a planned trilogy (Maybe More!) Clement and Dagena first appeared in the novel, 'Adalbert.'

About the Author

Craig R. Hipkins was born in Worcester, Massachusetts in 1968. He currently lives in North Carolina. Please visit his website at www.hipkinstwins.com. If you have enjoyed this book, please leave a review on Amazon or Goodreads.

Coming Soon!

Clement: The Templar's Treasure (Book # 3 in the Clement series)

Clement and Dagena return for another adventure. This time they journey to the fabled land of Vinland to seek the legendary treasure of the Knights Templar. Along the way, they must overcome Clement's nemesis, the diabolical Sven the Terrible!

www.ingramcontent.com/pod-product-compliance
Lightning Source LLC
Chambersburg PA
CBHW071923150726

47999CB00001B/76